REBEL DAWN

A Civil War Novel

DAVID HEALEY

INTRACOASTAL

REBEL DAWN

By David Healey

Print edition ISBN 978-0-9674162-9-8

Cover design by Juan Padron.

BISAC Subject Headings:

FIC014000 FICTION/Historical

FIC032000 FICTION/War & Military

"Where are the vaunts, and the proud boasts with which you went forth? Where are your banners, and your bands of music, and your ropes to bring back prisoners? The sun rises, but shines not."
—Walt Whitman

CHAPTER ONE

BALTIMORE, APRIL 1861

TOM FLYNN STEPPED out onto the street that April morning and could hardly believe his eyes and ears. He had ducked into a saloon earlier for a beer and some oysters and now felt pleasantly full. His thoughts had turned to a woman he knew on Fort Avenue, wondering if she might be desiring some company. On the street, there were the usual salty smells from Baltimore harbor and the sights of damp cobblestones strewn with the soggy stumps of cigars, shards of broken green and pale blue glass that sparkled like cheap jewelry in the sunlight, and a stray cat bouncing away with its prize of a fish head. But none of that was what held Flynn's attention at the moment.

Like the sudden appearance of a spring thunderstorm, now the street was filled with shouting people, some of the men waving clubs and knives, calling out, "Death to Yankees!" Ominously, a few carried guns in one hand and whiskey bottles in the other. A whiskey-sodden woman stumbled by, screeching like a crazed harpy that Lincoln was a devil.

Flynn rocked back on his heels, taking it all in. Considering that he had been at various times a soldier, a prizefighter, and a gambler, there were not many sights that surprised him anymore, but the appearance of these rioters on the streets of Baltimore was something altogether different. He flexed his broad shoulders and waggled the fingers of his powerful hands.

Flynn was a big man, well over six feet tall, broad-shouldered, with the dark hair and eyes that some called Black Irish. He was handsome at first glance, but then you noticed the tiny scars of a fighter around his eyes and the nose that had been broken and reset crookedly. His clothes were like that, too, looking fashionable enough until you spotted a few buttons that were missing and what might be a bullet hole in the sleeve. He seemed to have a look of perpetual amusement on his face, a wry smile dancing on his thin lips, even in the boxing ring or at the card table. Anger was a fool's errand. For Flynn, life was a story with a funny twist, a game where you were better off ignoring the rules if you wanted to win. One thing for sure, he was going to tell his own story, and he'd do his damnedest to beat you at any game, and usually did.

The sight of the rioters set him on edge. Had the world gone mad?

A man reeled drunkenly into Flynn. He shouted up into Flynn's face, spittle flying, "Get out of my way!"

Flynn might have begged his pardon, but he wasn't in the mood. He took the man by the elbow and flung him into the crowded street like he was skipping a stone into the sea. The man tumbled and rolled helplessly, trampled under many feet. Quickly, Flynn walked away from the shouts of outrage. Mobs were dangerous things to provoke.

At first, he tried to move in the opposite direction from the crowd flowing down Pratt Street, but it was like swimming against the stream. He turned around and allowed himself to be carried along on the current.

Someone broke into song. The tune was "Maryland, My Maryland" by James Ryder Randall that had become popular as wartime tensions built. Flynn didn't know the words, but no matter—several voices around him sang along:

. . .

THE DESPOT'S heel is on thy shore
Maryland! My Maryland!

HE HADN'T PAID much attention to news about the outbreak of the war, being busy with other pursuits, such as drinking and gambling, not to mention the occasional visit to one of the women who kept rooms above the waterfront saloons.

It was a lifestyle that suited him fine, but as they say, no man is an island. There had been signs and warnings that Flynn had scarce believed. It seemed impossible to him that the United States of America could be torn asunder. But all through the winter and spring, rumors had flown that blue-coated soldiers would be marching into the South to quell the rebellion.

Rebellion. There was no other word for it. South Carolina had seceded back in December, but in Flynn's opinion, they were all mad-eyed rebels—and far away. However, Virginia had left the Union just two days ago. It was a toss of the coin as to whether or not Maryland would follow. Like it or not, the mob was proof that the war had arrived on Baltimore's doorstep.

Soon, the source of the mob's outrage became apparent. He watched in amazement as a neat column of blue-coated soldiers marched down the street. For the mob, the sight of federal troops was like waving a red flag at a bull.

"These Yankees are on their way to protect the capital!" someone shouted. "Don't let them through!"

"Go home, Yankees! You're not wanted here!"

It seemed like madness to provoke an entire city by marching troops through the streets, but Flynn knew that the Federal troops had little choice. The railroad tracks did not go all the way through the city. There was a depot where the rails from the north ended. A few blocks away, there was a depot where the tracks south began. Passengers had to walk or take a carriage across town to connect from one depot to the other. These Union volunteers from Massachusetts were marching through Baltimore to reach the depot where they could board the train carrying them to Washington City.

Confronted by the surging mob, the soldiers were forced to halt. The two opposing forces had reached an impasse.

An officer shouted, "Fix bayonets!"

Steel flashed in the spring sun as long, gleaming bayonets were affixed to the soldiers' muskets. He had to admit that the soldiers looked frightening and intimidating. It was looking as if the troops might try to clear the streets using force.

Instead of clearing the streets, the mob responded by jeering and booing the soldiers.

The ugly crowd bubbled like a pot of crab soup about to boil over.

Flynn didn't like the looks of the situation. He edged away from the gathering storm until he stood at the fringes of the mob. However, the sheer number of people pouring toward the scene from all directions kept him from escaping. He did his best to keep out of the way.

That's when he saw a young black mother, holding a small boy by the hand. She was very light-skinned, most likely what the locals called a mulatto, or mixed race. Like Flynn, they had been caught in the wrong place at the wrong time by this mob. But Flynn wasn't a target for the mob—as far as they knew, he was one of them, another secessionist. On the other hand, the mulatto woman and her child were a target for the crowd's wrath. Hadn't this business about slavery brought the Union troops here? Slave or free, black or mulatto, it was all the same to them.

The woman was trying to skirt the mob and make her way down the street, but the mob was having none of it.

"Get those two!" someone shouted. "It's all their fault, them and their kind!"

A ring of angry Baltimoreans surrounded the woman, cutting off any hope of escape. He took a step toward them, then stopped. This wasn't any of his business. Maybe he ought to keep out of it. But then again, keeping out of things never had been in Flynn's nature.

Before Flynn could make up his mind, he was distracted by a crescendo of angry shouts rising from the rioters nearest the troops. Despite their fixed bayonets, the troops had not been ordered to use them. In fact, their muskets remained shouldered rather than being leveled at the crowd.

Flynn frowned. The soldiers' reluctance to use force had emboldened the mob.

It was unlike anything that he had seen before. More rioters were being drawn like a moth to a flame. He saw an empty whiskey bottle fly through the air and strike an officer. He stumbled and put his hand to his head, where he now had an ugly gash in his forehead.

More objects began to be hurled at the troops in the front row. Flynn watched as a drunken civilian bent down and worked thick fingers around a paving stone to pull it from the street itself. With a furious shout, he hurled it toward the approaching troops. The stone struck with far more force than the bottle had. This time, a soldier fell.

Unfortunately for the troops, the mob had an endless supply of pavers. He saw more people stoop down and claw the stones free from the street, then throw them at the troops. Soon, the air was raining stones.

Ominously, the soldiers finally leveled their muskets at the mob. The rioters did not back down, but seemed to become more frenzied by the threat. More objects filled the air, hurled at the troops, along with insults.

Nearby, he heard more shouting from the circle of rioters surrounding the mulatto woman. He was surprised to see a young man —in truth, he was not much more than a boy—waving a cane sword at the crowd, forcing them back. The mother and child cowered behind him. He was succeeding in keeping the crowd away, but for how long?

Some in the crowd carried cudgels, knives, or even guns. The lad would soon be overwhelmed.

Flynn headed in that direction. He should have known better, but he could not seem to stop himself. The lad was doing the right thing, and he shouldn't be doing it alone. Once they had overwhelmed the young man, the mob would tear the young mother and child to pieces.

Flynn shoved his way through the ring surrounding the boy, grabbing people and tossing them roughly aside. He joined the young man and stood shoulder to shoulder with him.

"What's your plan, lad?" he asked.

"I don't have a plan!" the young man responded. At first glance, he was even younger than Flynn had thought, with no more than peach fuzz covering his chin, in stark contrast to the bearded men looming around them.

"Then we'll make it up as we go along."

The only weapon that Flynn possessed was a derringer, but he kept that in his pocket for now. His presence seemed to keep the mob at bay. He was a good half a foot taller than anyone else. Despite his gambler's suit, it was clear that Flynn had shoulders like an oak beam and arms to match.

One of the rioters made the mistake of stepping forward, shouting insults. Flynn's fist sent him sprawling. Beside him, the lad's thin blade darted this way and that. One of the rioters howled as the point stung him.

But the crowd was growing. The mother hugged her little boy protectively and pressed against the brick wall behind them as if hoping it would magically open and give them a route to safety.

Two men launched themselves at Flynn. His fist stopped one. He blocked a punch with his left arm and stomped on the man's toes, making him howl. While the man was distracted, he hit him in the ear. Flynn had learned a long time ago that it didn't pay to fight fair.

"We can't do this forever, lad," Flynn said.

"What about the police? Won't they help us?"

"Are you daft? This is Baltimore and those are federal troops. It's a safe bet that the police are the ones leading the riot."

"What are we supposed to do?"

"We'll have to make a run for it. When I give the word, you help the young lady and I'll try to push our way through. If nothing else, maybe I can buy you some time to get away."

It wasn't much of a plan and Flynn didn't like their chances—especially *his* chances. One on one, or even two on one, he felt that he could fight his way through. But if the mob rushed him, it would all be over in moments.

As it turned out, they got a lucky break as the riot against the troops turned even more violent.

Bombarded by bottles and paving stones, the battered troops finally seemed to have had enough. A musket fired, and then another. Then came a ragged volley. Smoke and screams filled the street.

Some of the soldiers, to their credit, had fired over the heads of the crowd, intending to warn them off. But not all of the soldiers had done so, aiming directly into the crowd instead. Several crumpled bodies now lay in the street.

But the mob wasn't defenseless. Several guns fired back at the soldiers. One or two went down, but the rest were busy reloading for another volley.

The distraction created their best chance of escape.

"Now!" Flynn shouted.

The young man took the mother by the shoulder and pulled her and the boy in Flynn's wake as he bulled through the crowd, scattering the surprised rioters.

Farther away, another volley of shots rang out. Flynn kept pushing, glancing back once to make sure that the lad and the mother were still with him.

The musket fire and return gunshots created pandemonium. He looked back and caught a glimpse of a body, blood flowing down the cobblestones. A little beyond that, he saw another dead rioter. He saw a muzzle flash and the puff of smoke from a weapon, but it was impossible to tell if the shot had come from one of the soldiers or from the rioters. More scattered shots followed. Some people ran away, while others streamed toward the fight. People shoved and pushed in all directions.

Flynn took advantage of the confusion, leaving behind the small mob that had surrounded them. His plan was to head toward the waterfront, where the mob had not yet reached.

They soon arrived at the wharves of Baltimore harbor. Nobody was chasing them—for now. The mob was focused on battling the Federal troops.

He wasn't sure how much longer the wharves would remain a refuge. Flynn had been correct that it was actually the Baltimore police and even some city officials leading the mob, outraged by the interference of Federal soldiers. The entire city remained a powder keg. You were either with the mob, or against them. Flynn worried that he might be recognized later for having interfered to help the mother and the young man. He tended to stand out in a crowd. He might have gotten off the street, but the room that he'd taken was back in the direction of Pratt Street. He'd never make it.

They heard more gunfire in the distance. The shouting came closer.

"This way," said a black dockworker, who seemed to have some experience in knowing when someone was running from trouble. He nodded at the young mother with might have been recognition, or simply acknowledgment of her predicament. Several more men stood with him, armed with ax handles and hammers. Many of the men were skilled boatbuilders responsible for Baltimore's fleet of skipjacks and majestic clipper ships. "You'll be safe here. If the mob comes this way, we've got boats to get away."

Several of the men defending the wharves glared at Flynn and the young man, starting toward them threateningly. The young man was empty-handed, having lost his sword cane in the earlier scuffle.

"Leave them alone!" cried the mother. "They helped me."

The men eyed them with suspicion, but didn't attack. Still, Flynn felt like he was caught between a rock and a hard place.

The mention of boats gave Flynn an idea. He'd had enough of Baltimore and its mobs. Looking around, he spotted a steamer at the dock, getting ready to make way. Smoke poured from the stacks as it built up steam. Crewmen hurried to free the lines securing the vessel to the pier. Evidently, the sound of the rioting had encouraged the captain to set sail before the chaos reached the waterfront.

Flynn ran up the gangplank just in time, followed by the young man. He had almost forgotten about him until he heard him pounding up the gangplank after him.

"I don't have much money," the young man said, panting, once they were safely aboard the ship.

"I'll pay the fare," Flynn said. "It's the least I can do. You saved that young woman's life. A favor deserves a favor."

"Where are we going?"

Flynn laughed. "I don't care if we're sailing to Hades, lad, as long as it's away from here!"

CHAPTER TWO

ONCE THE STEAMER BEGAN TO GAIN SPEED AND LEAVE THE DOCK behind, heading out of Baltimore harbor and into the Chesapeake Bay, Flynn started to relax. The breeze was fresh, and the steamer rocked slightly in the swell on the open bay.

They had clearly been fleeing trouble, but the captain and crew asked no questions. In fact, the captain offered what passed for advice.

"If I were you, I wouldn't show my face in Baltimore again anytime soon," the man said. He added with a laugh, "If you do, it's a coffin you'll be needing, not a steamship ticket!"

Pointedly, the captain had not enquired as to what the trouble had been about. After all, the Baltimore waterfront had long been a crossroads between North and South. This steamer was heading down the bay, but others carried passengers north, through the Chesapeake and Delaware Canal up to Philadelphia.

There were even rumors that more than one runaway slave had taken the desperate step of having himself nailed inside a box and shipped to Philadelphia as deck cargo, surrounded by slave traders who leaned against the box and smoked cigars. The passengers often included abolitionists alongside the slave traders. To avoid trouble, the captain of a Chesapeake Bay steamer learned not to ask many questions. It was bad for business, and possibly for his health.

Flynn turned to the young man who stood beside him at the rail.

"What's your name, lad?" Flynn asked.

"Jay Warfield."

"Tom Flynn," he said, and put out his hand. They shook.

"You sound Irish."

"Aye," Flynn said. He paused, wondering what the young man would say about that, but the lad made no comment. "You have soft hands, Mr. Warfield. That means you're not a farmer. You are a young gentleman, I take it?"

Jay had been slumped over the ship's rail, looking out at the passing waterfront filled with buy boats and oyster skipjacks, but he drew himself up straight. He was still several inches shorter than Flynn. "I am a soldier—or I will be, soon."

"Is that right? You could have joined up with those Union troops back there. It seemed to me that they could have used the help."

Jay stood straighter still as he announced, "I am joining the Confederate army."

"The Confederacy? Considering how you helped that young woman back there, are you sure that you're signing up for the right side?"

"I have my reasons. State's rights, for one. What I don't believe in is attacking young mothers and children."

"Even a mulatto?"

The young man didn't hesitate. "Even a mulatto."

Flynn nodded. He'd been ready to write off the young man with the soft hands and the fine suit as foolhardy, but he now reconsidered. Jay Warfield had nearly been stomped to death by a mob while standing up for someone whom he didn't even know. In Flynn's book, that took some sand.

"Are you even old enough to sign up for any army? You have to be eighteen, you know."

"Sure, I'm old enough."

Flynn shook his head doubtfully. "You're not a very good liar, Jay. How old are you, really?"

"Seventeen—or I will be in two months."

"You do realize that Maryland remains in the Union, even if most people in Baltimore would seem to prefer otherwise. You'll need to cross the Potomac River into Virginia to sign up."

"I know that."

"How do you propose to get yourself to Virginia?"

"Others have done it. I suppose that I can, too."

Flynn didn't doubt it—the lad had faced off against an angry mob, after all. "Here's a bit of advice, lad. Keep your goal of joining the Confederacy to yourself. You don't want to end up in jail—or worse yet, you could find yourself in a blue uniform. The so-called recruiters don't always give a young man on his own much choice when they're looking to fill their quota."

"I'd rather die before I put on a blue uniform, Mr. Flynn," Jay said.

Flynn thought about that. "Those are strong words, lad. Your family must own slaves."

"A few," Jay admitted. "My family has a farm near Ellicott's Mills. They're treated well."

"If you say so." Flynn might not have taken sides in this war, but he was no fan of slavery. It didn't sit right with him, the thought of one man owning another. Anyone who was Irish by birth understood what it meant to be under the boot heel of someone else.

"I am not fighting for slavery," Jay said. "My father says they'll all be freed in a few years anyhow, one way or another."

"Then why the Confederacy?" Flynn added, "*Faith, as you say, there's small choice in rotten apples.*"

"That sounds like Shakespeare. You are full of surprises, Mr. Flynn."

"Flynn suits me fine. But you didn't answer my question. Why join the Confederacy?"

Jay shifted from foot to foot, taking his time answering. When he finally spoke, the answer poured out in a rush. "My older brother joined the Union. I hate him, you see, for a terrible wrong that he has done me, but he enlisted before I could settle accounts against him. If I can't fight him, then I will at least fight *against* him. Besides, there is nothing for me at home now."

"Why would anyone hate his brother that much?"

Again, Jay's answer was slow in coming. "He stole away the girl that I loved."

"Aye, that's a bad turn."

"They are to be married, you see. My father already gave his approval. They are to marry as soon as he returns home from the war, and we all know it won't last long. I am joining the Confederacy in hopes that I may get him in my musket sights."

"What does your father think of that?"

"I left him a letter explaining myself."

"You ran away from home?"

"I suppose I did, when you put it that way," Jay said. "What else was I to do? What about you? Which side are you going to join?"

"I don't plan on joining either side."

Jay seemed to be a serious young man, with the weight of being wronged on his shoulders—at least as he saw it—but for the first time, he smiled. "Good luck with that, Mr. Flynn. Don't you know that the whole country has gone as mad as a box of frogs?"

* * *

FLYNN AVOIDED THE OTHER PASSENGERS, and the rest of the trip to Annapolis was uneventful. Although it was Maryland's capital, Annapolis remained a sleepy waterfront town when the legislature wasn't in session. Like many old Chesapeake Bay towns, it had a genteel or even English atmosphere, with neat brick homes, cobble-stoned streets, and village greens shaded by old oaks and sycamores.

Maryland's legislature would have voted to secede from the Union if President Lincoln had not taken the step of arresting all of the pro-secession state senators and delegates. The leaders were now impris-oned at Fort McHenry in Baltimore harbor. Ironically, some of those imprisoned were descendants of those who had fought against the British there during the War of 1812, including the nephew of Francis Scott Key, who had scratched out his famous poem, "The Star-Span-gled Banner," while witnessing that fight.

Lincoln's actions had secured Maryland and meant that the nation's capital city would not be an island in a secessionist state. Still, it made for an uneasy situation.

With Baltimore such a hotbed of pro-Southern copperheads, sending more troops through the city would be a disaster, as witnessed by the riot that Flynn had seen. City officials had gone north of Baltimore to burn the railroad bridges, claiming that they were trying to prevent more unrest, although it was an open question as to whether they were actually trying to thwart the Union itself.

Union troops would soon pour into Annapolis, taking transports from Philadelphia, through the Chesapeake & Delaware Canal, then down Chesapeake Bay to avoid the railroad into Baltimore. That city would soon be nicknamed, "Mob town."

For now, the scenic streets of Annapolis remained quiet, an onslaught of troops still being days away. Inviting though the town might be, he had no intention of staying. Instead, he meant to return to Washington City.

From Annapolis, a rail line ran right to the nation's capital and Flynn booked passage for himself and Jay.

"You'll have an easier time getting to Virginia from Washington City than from Annapolis," Flynn had pointed out. "It's also a short trip home from there, right out the Washington Road, should you change your mind about enlisting."

"I'm not going home."

"Suit yourself."

The train trip to Washington was relatively uneventful. After stepping off onto the station platform, Flynn started to walk away, then stopped, realizing that he'd left young Jay Warfield standing there alone as if he hadn't a friend in the world.

With a sigh, Flynn turned around. "Lad, do you have a place to stay?"

"I'll find something."

"You might as well come along with me and get something to eat."

That's just what they did, dining in the hotel where Flynn had managed to find a room—which wasn't easy or cheap, given the sudden demand prompted by the war.

Jay ate with the gusto of a hungry teenage boy. Once he had

finished, he looked around the crowded dining room with ill-concealed awe. The diners consisted of Union officers, well-dressed businessmen, and a few women who were not likely to be their wives.

"This is the farthest I've ever been from home," Jay said quietly. "I don't have much money. Where will I go?"

Flynn barely looked up from his plate of oysters. "You can sleep on my floor, lad."

For better or for worse, Flynn realized that he had taken the lad under his wing.

He should have known better, he supposed, but hadn't others done the same for him? He smiled, thinking of old Father McGlynn, who had taken Flynn in and taught him a thing or two about the world when he was still wet behind the ears. He owed the man a debt, but it would be impossible to ever pay him back because the priest was long since dead and gone. Instead, he would take in this young fool in tribute to his old friend.

* * *

FLYNN SAW how quickly the city had changed. Washington was now a city at war and its citizens were sharply divided. Tempers flared on both sides. It wasn't unusual for gangs of drunken men to go looking for trouble. Unfortunately for Flynn, trouble always seemed to have a way of finding him.

He was walking along the street when a band of drunken blue-coated soldiers went past. Flynn was careful to keep his eyes elsewhere, for all the good it did him.

"You there! Why aren't you in uniform?" demanded a burly soldier with sergeant's stripes on his sleeves. "Big as you are, I hope you ain't a coward!"

"The war will be over so fast that you won't need my help," Flynn said, smiling genially.

"Come along with us and I'll see that you're signed up."

"I don't think so."

"Hold on." The sergeant scowled, reeling a bit. He was a little worse for wear from drink. "You ain't one of those secessionists, are you?"

Now, the other soldiers had taken an interest in the exchange. They began to circle like a pack of dogs. Flynn curled his hands into fists and squared his shoulders. If they wanted trouble, they would get it.

But to his surprise, it didn't come to that. One of the men pointed to a building up the street and shouted in outrage, "They're flying a Confederate flag!"

Flynn looked to where the soldier was pointing. Sure enough, a homemade "Stars and Bars" was hanging from an upstairs window. Feelings ran so strong in these early days of the war that some Southern sympathizers thought nothing of provoking the bluecoats.

The angry soldiers swarmed up the street and stormed inside the building. They dragged out an older man, who cursed them.

"Call me a traitor? You're the traitors!"

But this was not to be the old man's day. It was his bad luck that a roof was being repaired nearby with tar. Despite the protests of the roofers, who were about to carry the tar up a ladder, the soldiers seized the tar.

Their intent was clear, and the man they had captured cried out in alarm and tried to get away. For his efforts, he was punched and kicked to the ground.

That made the soldiers' task all that easier. They poured the bucket of tar over his head. The tar wasn't hot enough to burn, but the man still cried out piteously as the black substance flowed from his head, down across his face, and coated his upper body. The man tried to protest through the sticky, suffocating mess.

Flynn took a step toward the group, but stopped himself. If he intervened, he would very likely end up like this fool who thought that he could display a Southern flag with impunity on a street filled with drunken soldiers. He had gotten lucky with the Baltimore mob. He wasn't sure that he wanted to push his luck more than necessary.

The soldiers then threw handfuls of feathers at the man from a pillow that they had found in the house. He was forced to straddle a rail and then carried along the street until the soldiers got tired of it and dumped the man to the ground, where he lay moaning.

Roaring with laughter, the soldiers stood around and watched.

Feeling like a coward, Flynn hurried in the opposite direction before the soldiers got bored and went looking for their next victim.

Washington had once been a congenial city, a mixing bowl of opinions. Now, not so much. The battle lines had been drawn between North and South.

Maybe young Jay Warfield was right. How much longer could he straddle those lines without choosing sides?

* * *

THREE DAYS after his return to the Union capital, Flynn was surprised when a message arrived from Mrs. Rose Greenhow, summoning him to an audience. He did not know her personally, but he did know of her reputation as a Southern rabble-rouser. Whole newspaper articles had been devoted to her, and Flynn had read one or two of them. Her name had become synonymous with the loose organization of Confederate sympathizers operating in Washington City. He should have tossed the note away. That would have been the smart thing to do. The last thing he needed was more trouble.

However, his curiosity has been piqued.

He decided to ask an acquaintance about her. Noah Sloane wrote for the Washington Star newspaper, so was privy to all the news that never made it into print. Sloane was a terrible card player, but he was genial enough and shrugged off his losses as long as you bought the man a drink now and then. Flynn was convinced that the man kept at his poor card playing because of the gossip he picked up.

"What do you know of this Rose Greenhow?" Flynn asked, once he explained that she wanted to meet with him.

Sloane raised an eyebrow. "She's a secessionist. Everyone knows it. There's even a rumor that she actively spies for Richmond."

"What does she want with me?"

"It won't be to serve the Union, that's for sure," Sloane said, clearly amused. "Oh, and be careful—her house is being watched. You go and see her, and you'll be listed as a spy, sure as a horse gets a saddle."

Flynn tucked the note away, thinking it over.

CHAPTER THREE

FLYNN MIGHT HAVE IGNORED THE REQUEST TO MEET WITH THE notorious Confederate spy Rose Greenhow, but curiosity got the better of him. Whatever the woman wanted, he decided to hear her out. Also, Mrs. Greenhow was supposed to be rich. Maybe whatever she had in mind might put some money in Flynn's pocket.

The truth was that he found himself at loose ends—he had planned to spend some time in Baltimore, making money where he could by playing cards in the waterfront saloons, where oystermen flush with pay were eager to try their luck. He felt right at home in the rough-and-tumble atmosphere, rooms were cheap, and the rewards were worthwhile. However, those plans had been cut short with the start of the war and the riot.

Consequently, he was short of funds. The cost of the hotel in Washington, along with meals and whiskey, was quickly eating up his money. It didn't help that the sudden demand prompted by the war had caused a huge increase in the price of everything.

Then there was Jay. Still sleeping on Flynn's floor and eating meals with him at the hotel, Jay had offered to contribute.

"I have a little money," he'd said, opening his palm to reveal half a dozen silver dollars. A guilty look crossed Jay's face. "I'm afraid that I took the coins from my father, but I shall pay him back."

"Keep your money, lad," Flynn said gruffly. "Always carry it with you and hide it well. Slip those coins into a seam of your coat if you can. There may come a time when you need that money."

The truth was, in part, that Flynn was too proud to accept the coins from the boy. His card-playing expedition to Baltimore had been cut short and he'd had a run of bad luck in Washington City, where the stakes were higher and the players were more skilled. Flynn wasn't the only gambler working the tables at the hotels. There was always prize-fighting, which had put food in his belly before, but he preferred to use his head for something besides a punching bag.

Something would turn up. Flynn was a man used to living by his wits, after all. Maybe this summons from Mrs. Greenhow would be the opportunity that he was looking for.

Passing through the street, he gave a squad of blue-coated soldiers a wide berth. As he had already discovered, it wasn't unusual for troops to heckle men who were out of uniform.

He had no intention of putting on a blue uniform—or any uniform, for that matter. The worst pay of all would be soldiering, which he planned to avoid at all costs. He had been a soldier before, fighting for the Pope in the Italian wars, and that experience had been enough for him. Like Jay, he had been eager to join up for that fight. Having seen war, he was in no hurry to see it again.

He made his way through the busy city to the address that he had been given. As he walked, he was amazed by the changes in the city.

A few short months ago, visitors to Washington City would have encountered a sleepy town. The stretch of Pennsylvania Avenue between the Capitol and the White House was weedy in places, even with small bushes growing up in the center of the muddy lane. The broad avenue rarely saw much traffic when Congress was not in session. Pigs wallowed in the muddy places and chickens scratched at the sides of the avenue.

That had quickly changed as squadrons of cavalry trampled the weeds, making a clear road through the city. The pigs and the mud had remained, however.

Where he could, Flynn used the wooden sidewalk to keep the mud and horse droppings off his shoes. Up ahead, he saw more troops approaching and he hunched his shoulders and adopted a stooped appearance, hoping to escape notice. That was easier said than done because at any given time, Flynn was usually the biggest man on the street.

Despite his efforts to blend in, he felt curious eyes upon him. Any man of a certain age was generally expected to be donning a uniform. It was quickly becoming apparent that men who still wore civilian clothes were thought to be medical rejects, louts and horse traders, spies—or worse yet, cowards.

Flynn had no doubts about his personal courage and felt no need to prove anything to anyone. From his outward appearance, no one was going to believe that Flynn suffered from some weakness of health or nerve. He didn't look like a coward and he lacked the shifty eyes of a horse trader.

But being an able-bodied man who wasn't in uniform definitely left open the possibility that he was a spy. The curious eyes upon him made Flynn uncomfortable and he hurried on toward his destination.

As it turned out, Mrs. Greenhow lived in a stately home that towered three stories above the street, taller than it was wide. A low iron fence surrounded the front of the house—more than simply decorative, the fence kept the feral hogs away. It was a substantial house, similar to the fancy homes of the wealthy found from Richmond to Philadelphia.

Perhaps it was only his imagination, but he thought that he had seen a corner flick back from one of the downstairs curtains as he approached. It was a furtive movement. Was he expected, or was someone inside keeping watch?

He couldn't help but glance around, wondering who might be watching the house. That man standing on the corner with no particular purpose, perhaps? Or was it the weary woman with her worn clothes, sitting on the steps nearby? In either case, he was sure that his presence was noted.

Washington was now a Northern city, and it was no secret as to which side Mrs. Rose O'Neal Greenhow favored. She was a native

Marylander, having been born on a modest plantation in Port Tobacco, a waterfront village located at a bend in the Potomac River, in the last year of the second war with the British. The British had marched into Washington and burned it down that same year, but of course, she was too young to remember.

When she was a young girl on their farm, her father had been murdered by a slave. Given her personal history, it was hardly a surprise that she had lent her support to the Confederacy.

Now a wealthy widow, she might very well be Washington City's most notorious spy. Yet she was allowed to operate her spy ring—for now. Flynn was sure there was a certain value for the Yankees in knowing who came and went from Mrs. Greenhow's house.

Hat in hand, he knocked on the door and was admitted. The interior felt cool and hushed, as if the turmoil in the wartime city streets had not yet reached these rooms and halls. Looking around at the furnishings, Flynn was impressed. He had rarely been allowed through the front door of such a house. Clearly, Mrs. Greenhow was a woman of substance. Old oil paintings decorated the walls and rich carpets covered the floors. The furniture was highly polished and an expensive grandfather's clock ticked in the entryway.

He followed a servant into the parlor.

A woman rose to greet him. He had never met Mrs. Greenhow, but there was no doubt that this was her. Well-dressed, her hair drawn back tightly in a way that amplified her striking gaze, the reputed spy looked him up and down.

The eyes did not reveal anything other than cool appraisal. If she was glad to see him, or curious, it didn't show. Flynn thought that Mrs. Greenhow would have made a formidable card player.

"Ma'am," he said, working to suppress his brogue. He suspected that Mrs. Greenhow, despite being an O'Neal originally, was not one to favor the Irish. That would have made her like most established people in Washington City.

He soon learned that Mrs. Greenhow was nothing if not direct. She had all the impatience typical of the rich. The servant was dismissed without Flynn being offered so much as a glass of water.

She did not even bother with small talk, but announced, "I think that you will do."

"Beggin' yer pardin, ma'am?" Flynn silently cursed himself for slipping into his brogue, which he had a tendency to do when nervous.

"Mr. Flynn, I want you to go to Richmond and bring home a friend."

Standing there in the parlor, Flynn considered the request. He had no particular allegiance to the North or South. Richmond or Boston—it was all the same to Flynn. For him, it was all about the money. How much was the woman offering? But he wasn't ready to ask just yet.

"Richmond is now in the Confederacy, ma'am," he pointed out. Though scarcely more than one hundred miles apart, the two cities were now separated by more than distance. "The lines have been drawn."

"I am aware of that."

"It's dangerous work," he said.

"I'm not asking you to be a spy, Mr. Flynn. That *would* be dangerous. No, I am asking you to undertake a rescue mission."

"Does your friend want to be rescued?"

"Perhaps not yet, but no matter. You see, some people must be saved from themselves."

Flynn snorted. "Did your son run away and join the Confederacy?"

"If I had a son, I would hope that is exactly what he would do, unlike my son-in-law, who is a Union officer," she said. "No, I'm afraid that this is more complicated. I have a dear friend who is playing at being a spy. She is in Richmond, and I want you to bring her home safely to Washington City."

"What if she doesn't want to come home?"

"Then you must protect her until she does come home."

Flynn had to admit that he was now curious, if not quite sold on the proposal.

"Who is this friend that you care so much about?"

"Her name is Anna Ella Carroll," she said, then paused to see if the name registered at all with Flynn.

It did not. "Never heard of her."

"Most haven't, and yet, you see, she is a very important personage. She is a confidante of none other than President Lincoln."

Flynn raised an eyebrow. "Then why doesn't Mr. Lincoln send for her?"

"I am sure that he has other concerns at the moment."

"You may be right about that," Flynn said, thinking of the rioters and the divided country. The fate of a woman playing at being a spy would be more than he could concern himself with.

"Miss Carroll comes from an esteemed family. Like me, she is a Marylander. In fact, her father was the governor of Maryland. Her great-grandfather signed the Declaration of Independence. She knows everyone of importance in this city and well beyond."

"A socialite."

"A politician, you might say. A woman of great conviction and intelligence," Greenhow said. "She has written several articles, pamphlets, and books that have been quite influential."

"Then why haven't I heard of her?"

A haughty smile played over the woman's tight lips. "Are you much of a reader, Mr. Flynn? You may be familiar with her book, *Star of the West*? Perhaps you have read her famous pamphlet, *The Union of the States*?"

"No, I don't suppose that I've read those."

"Then you shall have to take my word for it when I say that she is a talented author. I do have to tell you that some of her work has not been favorable toward the Irish. I can hear the Emerald Isle in your voice. My people are also from Ireland, but somehow, Miss Carroll and I have remained friends."

"It won't be a problem for me, so long as it is not a problem for her."

"Let's hope that it won't be."

"How will I even know who I'm looking for? Richmond is not exactly a small city. Surely she won't be using her own name."

Mrs. Greenhow smiled winsomely. "Unfortunately, I don't believe that Miss Carroll will make any pretense about who she is, although I hope she has sense enough not to say *why* she is in Richmond."

"She's a fool if she doesn't understand the dangers. These are serious times, Mrs. Greenhow."

"You don't think I know that, Mr. Flynn? It's Miss Carroll that I'm worried about. Here is her picture." Mrs. Greenhow handed him a *carte de visite*. The image showed a plain, round-faced woman, not the sort to attract a second look from most men. The woman in the photograph seemed to be the opposite of Mrs. Greenhow. Though well-past the age of youthful beauty, Mrs. Greenhow remained a striking woman. It was clear that the woman portrayed in the *carte de visite* had never been anything of the sort. Then again, as Flynn well knew, a plain appearance could be an advantage in terms of fitting in and going unnoticed.

"Not much to look at," he said.

"Appearances can be deceiving, Mr. Flynn. Sometimes, at least. For example, you look like exactly what you are."

"And what might that be?"

"A rogue."

He started to hand back the *carte de visite*, but Mrs. Greenhow shook her head. "Keep it," she said.

"I haven't said that I'll accept the job."

"I suppose that I shouldn't have expected to appeal to your good nature and have you accept."

"I haven't taken a side in this war, Mrs. Greenhow."

"So you say, but you will have to choose soon enough." She paused. "Until then, what will it take to convince you to fetch my friend home, Mr. Flynn?"

"How much are you offering?"

"Five hundred dollars," she said. "Half now, and the rest upon Miss Carroll's safe return."

He stopped himself just in time from raising his eyebrows in surprise. It was a great deal of money and Flynn's first instinct was to accept immediately before this conniving spy changed her mind. But he waited a long moment first, thinking it over. Playing the hand that he'd been dealt. "Plus expenses," he said.

"Within reason. Let's say five dollars per day."

"I'll need a horse. I can't walk to Richmond."

"Very well," she said.

"You must really want this woman back." Flynn was thinking that it might not be Miss Carroll that she wanted, so much as any information that the woman could give her.

Mrs. Greenhow sighed. "Will you do it or not, Mr. Flynn?"

"Yes," he heard himself say.

Finally, Mrs. Greenhow stood. He wasn't surprised to see that she was tall. Even sitting down, she had given the impression of height. "Very well," she said. "I will have the money sent to your hotel, if that is all right."

Flynn couldn't see any reason why it wouldn't be. "That's fine."

"I will also give you a letter, entreating Miss Carroll to give up her foolishness and return with you."

"Do you think that will help?"

"I can be very convincing."

He snorted. "I'm sure of that."

"One more thing. If you are caught, I will deny knowing you. You cannot expect any help from me."

Flynn nodded and smiled coldly. "You should know that works both ways, ma'am."

"Fair enough, Mr. Flynn. As you said, these are dangerous times."

CHAPTER FOUR

HAVING REACHED AN AGREEMENT WITH THE SOUTHERN SPY, MRS. Rose O'Neal Greenhow, and having accepted the delivery of his money and the letter at the hotel, his next step was to make preparations. The fact that getting to Richmond might get him shot or hanged added some complications to the trip. It didn't help that he had the Yankees to worry about on one side of the Potomac, and the Confederates on the other.

He felt no worry, however, but only a sense of anticipation for the adventure at hand. Flynn liked having a purpose. He realized that he had only been biding his time here in Washington and he felt eager to move on. The war had created a great deal of excitement and Flynn's decision to keep out of it had left him feeling sidelined.

Also, he always had liked Richmond and knew many people there, so it would be good to see them. There was no telling when that might be possible again.

However, there was one complication that he hadn't counted upon.

"I'm going with you," Jay announced.

"Like hell you are, lad."

"Why not?"

"Because it's dangerous, that's why."

"I was going South to volunteer, anyhow. It's high time I did that. If you don't take me with you, I'll just go on my own."

"What, cross the Potomac and then make your way through trigger-happy Southern pickets on the other side? That's if the Union pickets on this side don't shoot you first. You'll never make it by yourself!"

"Then take me with you."

Flynn glared. It was clear that Jay Warfield belonged to that class of young man who was rarely told that he couldn't do something. "You are a stubborn, pig-headed lad, aren't you?"

Jay grinned. "I knew that you'd say I could go."

Flynn had always known that young Jay had intended to cross the Potomac. He had stated as much back in Baltimore. Flynn would have preferred for the lad to sit out the war, which promised to be a short one. Unfortunately, he knew what it meant to be a hot-blooded young man, eager to get into uniform and have adventures.

Flynn shrugged. Further argument was pointless. "Suit yourself."

With the secession of Virginia in late May, all Potomac River crossings had quickly been closed or come under guard on both sides. This meant that there was not one gauntlet to run, but two.

However, no one would ever manage to completely halt all travel between the two countries—the United States of America and the Confederate States of America. There was no shortage of smugglers and watermen willing to earn a few extra dollars. Whether or not they had taken sides, they were opportunists.

As it turned out, Flynn had no need for smugglers. Another packet arrived for him from Mrs. Greenhow. There was a federal pass allowing him safe passage via the so-called chain bridge across the Potomac. Although the bridge had once been suspended on huge chains—and had once collapsed under the weight of a cattle drive—it was now more solidly built of wood and brick but had retained its nickname of "chain bridge."

Arrival on the Southern shore might have been problematic, but the spy had foreseen that as well and also provided a Confederate pass for safe passage into Virginia.

Flynn was impressed. How she had obtained these passes was a mystery. He realized that Mrs. Greenhow was not a force to be taken lightly. He would do well to remember that.

It would be a simple enough matter now to cross the chain bridge. But as he had told Mrs. Greenhow, he had no plans to walk all the way to Richmond.

He soon found himself at a livery stable to which Mrs. Greenhow's messenger had directed him. In the growing heat, the smell of horses was strong. The owner of the livery stable turned out to be a little potbellied man with a coat to which a few bits of straw clung. He had a greedy glint in his eye.

"Two horses, huh? They're in short supply these days, what with the demand from the army. Why, I could get a double-eagle for a sway-backed mule, and that's the honest truth. I hope that you've got plenty of cash, mister."

"I'm afraid that I don't," Flynn said. "All that I've got is a name."

The livery stable owner raised his eyebrows at the mention of Mrs. Greenhow, but he certainly changed his tune. Without any mention of price, he produced a good-sized bay roan gelding for Flynn and a mare for the boy.

"I appreciate it," Flynn said. "How much?"

"I will settle up with our mutual friend later. The South appreciates it," the man said, giving Flynn a wink. Arrangements were made to hold the animals until Flynn came for them.

There was one more item to procure. Flynn had the small derringer that he kept in his coat pocket, but it was not suitable for riding into a war zone.

He found a shop selling firearms of all sorts to the fresh-faced Union troops. They had been issued weapons—usually outdated muskets, some of which had been converted from flintlocks to percussion cap weapons. It went without saying that many of the soldiers preferred to provide a sidearm of their own. In particular, the new-fangled repeating revolvers were popular with officers.

Again, demand was high with prices to match, but that didn't stop Flynn from picking out a new LeMat revolver that had been made in France. The weapon had an over-and-under barrel configuration, with the upper barrel firing nine shots from the revolver, and the bottom barrel firing a shotgun shell loaded with buckshot. Flynn was no great marksman, so he appreciated having nine chances to hit his target and a burst of buckshot for good measure.

Mrs. Greenhow was no good to him here, unlike the stable, and he paid hard cash for the pistol. He consoled himself by the thought that if he needed to sell it later, the pistol would fetch a good price as long as there was a war on.

When he showed the LeMat to Jay, the lad whistled. "That's a beauty, all right. But what about me? Don't I get a pistol?"

Flynn gave him the derringer. "Do you know how to shoot?"

"Well enough. Besides, from the looks of this thing I'll have to be so close that I can't possibly miss."

"Keep it close. There may come a time when you're glad to have it."

Even after their preparations were made and Flynn had the passes across the bridge in hand, he found himself reluctant to leave. Two days stretched into three, then four. Part of it had to do with the weather. After a hot start to spring, cooler weather and heavy rain had arrived. The road to Richmond would be muddy.

"We'll head South when it dries out," Flynn told Jay.

Curious about Anna Ella Carroll, who had some reputation as a writer, he tracked down one of her popular pamphlets. This one ranted about the danger of Irish immigrants who were loyal to the Pope in Rome, rather than the US Constitution. Flynn just shook his head at that. It seemed to him that there were several hundred thousand native-born Americans who weren't very loyal to the Constitution. In fact, they had gone off and started their own country.

Flynn put the rest of his time to use by playing cards. His run of bad luck continued.

That night, he was coming back to the hotel from a card game in which Flynn had foolishly lost twenty dollars. The rain kept the street mostly deserted, although a few other men hurried home through the downpour. He was going over the last hand in his head and didn't pay any attention to the two men approaching him on the dark, rainy street until it was too late.

They stopped in front of him, blocking his path, rain sluicing off the brims of their hats and obscuring their faces.

They were big men, with a violent look about them. Instantly, he was alert. It helped that he went easy on the whiskey when playing cards.

He gave a quick look over his shoulder, but lucky for him, there was nobody behind him. He'd left the new revolver back in his hotel room and he'd already given the derringer to Jay. He still had his boot knife, but that would do him no good if the men had pistols.

Flynn never minded a fight, but this had the look of an ambush. Others had passed this way just ahead of him, hurrying through the rainstorm, but had been left alone. These two appeared to have been waiting for him.

"Gentlemen," he said mildly, touching the rain-soaked brim of his hat. "You seem to be in my way."

"Are you Flynn?"

"Who's asking?"

"We have a message for you about the company you keep," one of the men said.

Flynn was sure that the man wasn't referring to the low-stakes card game that he'd just come from, or to his association with young Jay Warfield, for that matter. That left one possibility, as Flynn saw it. "What company is that?"

"A certain Southern lady," the man said. "Whatever you're doing for her, you'd be better off leaving it alone."

"Is that so? Well, thank you for the advice."

"You're Irish, huh? Listen, Irish. It ain't advice. Consider it an order."

Flynn bristled at the way that the man called him *Irish*. It was the same tone that the man might have used for words like *mud* or *manure*. He decided that he'd had enough. "Then we're done here, mister. Just to be clear, nobody tells me what to do."

He started around the men. He kept to their right. It would be harder for them to throw a punch. He kept his eyes on them and bunched his fist. He left his left hand open to grab a gun, should one appear.

He fully expected trouble. He wasn't disappointed.

Something flashed in the dim light and Flynn caught the gleam of a knife.

So that's how it was going to be.

The man lunged at him, but Flynn had already begun to pivot.

Still, he was a bit too slow. The other man was familiar with knives and shifted at the last instant in reaction to Flynn's pivot. Flynn felt a flash of pain as the sharp blade nicked him. He caught the man's wrist in his left hand and stepped to one side, using the man's own momentum to throw him into the street. He fell headlong into the mud.

Before the second man could react, Flynn's right fist lashed out and struck him square in the face. Even above the rain, Flynn heard the satisfying crunch of bone. The man went down, blood flowing from his broken nose. He put muddy hands to his face and lay there, groaning. Flynn figured this fellow was out of the fight.

By now, the man with the knife was getting to his knees. Mud dripped off the blade as the attacker shifted his grip to hold the knife up high, so that he could jab it down at Flynn. This wasn't the man's first knife fight.

Flynn started reaching for the knife tucked into his boot, but as it turned out, he didn't need it. The other man slipped on the wet street, falling to his knees again. Cursing, he started to get up.

That was as far as Flynn wanted him to get. His boot connected with the fellow's chin and the man fell face-first into the mud, unconscious.

Flynn reached down and tossed the knife away. Then he rolled the man over so that he wouldn't drown right there in the street. Several inches of rain had created a muddy slop.

Quickly, Flynn splashed away, wary of other attackers that might be waiting in the shadows. He managed to make it back to the hotel without encountering more trouble. In between glancing into dark doorways and alleys, Flynn had time to think things over.

He realized that he had been foolish to linger in Washington City. Every action that he'd taken, from visiting Mrs. Greenhow to receiving the passes, to buying horses, had been like a stone thrown into the calm surface of a pond.

Those ripples had not gone unnoticed, it seemed.

If Mrs. Greenhow and her Confederate friends had a long reach, the Union had a longer one here in Washington City. In President Lincoln's city, the Union could do as it pleased and lock them away. Mrs. Greenhow might have wealth and many powerful friends to protect her, but Flynn had no money and no allies.

If two men had been sent to warn him off or worse, leave him bleeding in the street, by tomorrow morning there might be half a dozen thugs—or even a detail of blue-coated soldiers sent to arrest him as a traitor. Flynn had no desire to spend the rest of the war in the Old Capitol Prison.

They might arrest that foolish boy as well.

It was time to leave Washington City and get on with what he was being paid to do—the sooner, the better.

He found Jay stretched out on the bed, reading. Previously, Flynn had made it clear that the bed was *his*, and the lad ought to content himself with his pallet on the floor. After all, Flynn was the one paying for the room. But that was now the least of his concerns.

Jay hurried to slide off the bed. "Sorry, you weren't here, so I—" He caught sight of the gash on Flynn's arm. His eyes went wide. "Are you all right? What happened?"

Flynn put his arm over the washing basin and poured some whiskey on the wound, flinched, then wrapped it tightly in a strip of cloth. The cut wasn't deep. He was lucky that the blade hadn't ended up buried in his guts.

"Just a scratch, lad. But I'm afraid that there may be worse to come, and next time I may not get off so easy."

"What do you mean, next time? Wasn't it a robber?"

"Not a robber. This was because of my meeting with Mrs. Greenhow."

Jay knew about the meeting, of course. He also knew that Mrs. Greenhow was a notorious Southern spy. Flynn could almost see the cogs turning in the lad's head as he nodded and said, "I see."

"Good. Now get your things. We're leaving."

"Leaving? When?"

"Right now."

"But where are we going?"

"Why, to Richmond, you daft lad. Isn't that where you've been wanting to go? Now's your chance. That is, unless you've changed your mind about going home."

"I'm not going home!"

"That's settled, then. Now hurry it up! I want to be well across that chain bridge before first light."

CHAPTER FIVE

BEFORE FIRST LIGHT, THEY HAD CLAIMED THEIR HORSES FROM THE livery stable and ridden hard for the crossing into Virginia. The rain had let up, but the trees still dripped and mud spattered their clothes.

Thanks to the passes provided by Rose Greenhow, getting across the chain bridge proved less difficult than Flynn had anticipated. The Union pickets on the northern side of the Potomac barely paid them any attention. On the Virginia side of the river, the guards seemed to welcome them as fellow Southerners. Some of the Confederates sat on the ground, their weapons nowhere in sight, while a bottle made the rounds despite the early hour. He thought that the Southerners were treating this like a carnival, rather than a war.

"It's good that you decided to secede yourselves," the Confederate officer said jovially, after he had looked over their passes. "You've come over to God's side."

"Well now," Flynn said. "Having just come from Washington City, I know for a fact that the Yankees think that God is on their side."

"They'll find out the hard way soon enough which side the Almighty is on," the officer said.

Flynn laughed and saluted the officer. He doubted that God was taking any sides in this fight. However, he wasn't going to start off their trip South by disagreeing with the officer.

As they rode away, Flynn said to Jay, "You could join up right here and now if you wanted. I'm sure these boys would be glad to have you. Then again, the first Union cavalry across that bridge is going to wipe them out."

"Let's ride south and see what happens," Jay replied. Seeing his first Confederate troops and the reality of becoming a soldier seemed to have sobered him quite a bit to the idea of joining up.

They rode south. Flynn was pleased with the horses. He had half expected the big bay roan to be half lame, but the livery had provided decent animals and decent saddles. Again, he supposed that they had the long reach of Mrs. Greenhow to thank for that.

The country that they passed through felt tense with a mixture of emotions. While the Confederate troops at the bridge had been welcoming enough, the citizens of this new nation kept their distance. On the one hand, there was an air of excitement over the arrival of the war, but mostly, there was a great deal of the suspicion that came naturally to country people. The farmers and residents of the small towns they passed kept a wary eye out for strangers. They seemed to be wondering whose side the riders were on. Flynn thought that it should have been obvious. After all, they were riding South.

"It's hard to believe the country is at war," Jay said. "My grandfather was born when we were still part of England. The United States didn't last long."

"This war has been a long time coming," Flynn replied. "The Founding Fathers passed along the slavery question for someone else to solve. We're solving it now with bayonets."

"The war isn't about slavery!"

"If you say so." Flynn shook his head. He wasn't going to argue politics. "What it all comes down to is that Americans don't appreciate what they have."

"What do you mean?" Jay sounded puzzled. "Aren't you an American?"

"Sure I am, or at least I am now, but don't forget that I was born in Ireland, where there's not exactly a lot of opportunity to be had. That's where people who were born Americans take what they have for granted."

"That's why we have to fight for freedom."

"What would you know about it, lad? When has the likes of young Jay Warfield ever been denied his so-called freedom? Did soldiers ever put you off your land? Did your family ever starve because the crop failed?"

"No," Jay said quietly. "I suppose not. Is that what happened to your people in Ireland?"

Flynn sighed, realizing how bitter he sounded. But he felt that he had to prove a point to Jay. "The Irish are kept under the thumb of the English. You see, that's one of the reasons I joined up to be a soldier. On the one hand, it was an opportunity for adventure. Also, a lot of us Irish thought that fighting for the Pope would give us an ally against the English. But we were mistaken about that."

"You were a soldier before?" Jay asked. "I didn't know that."

"I was a soldier, all right. Like some other Irish fools, I joined the Pope's army when he called for volunteers. I was young and wet behind the ears back then. Hell, I was a lot like *you*, lad."

"Tell me about being a soldier."

"There's not a lot to tell," Flynn said. This wasn't true, but he decided to give Jay the short version. "Mostly, it was a lot of marching, a lot of rain, being cold at night, and being terrified during the battles."

"*You* were terrified? I don't believe it. You don't seem like you're afraid of anything."

"Come your first battle, lad, you'll see what I mean. Only a fool wouldn't be terrified. It's how you act when you're terrified that matters."

"All right," Jay said, sounding uncertain.

"Anyhow, the battles didn't go very well for us. It wasn't the fault of our brigade. The Irish fought well. In fact, some of the officers are over here now, fighting for one side or the other. The trouble was that we weren't well supplied. Our generals also left something to be desired."

"The generals weren't Irish?"

"Italians. But Julius Caesar, they were not. It takes three things to be a good soldier. First, you need to have courage, no matter what. Second, you need decent weapons and supplies. Third, you need a good general. In my experience, it's a rare thing for a soldier to have all three. About the only thing that we had was courage."

Jay nodded, taking it all in. He seemed to have a lot of questions and Flynn shared a few stories about his time in the Battalion of St. Patrick, made up of Irish and Irish-American volunteers.

When he had finished, Flynn snorted. "You still want to be a soldier?"

"I'm not going back home, if that's what you mean," Jay said. "I don't see how I have much choice now. Besides, my brother is fighting for the Union. He's a scoundrel. If I can meet him on the battlefield and prove who is the best man, so much the better."

"Be careful what you wish for, lad," Flynn said. "You may get your wish all too soon."

After that, they rode on for a while in silence, the horses moving at an easy pace.

Flynn thought about what Jay had said about hating his brother. All over a woman—a girl, really. It all sounded foolish to him.

Lads who were Jay's age tended to be hot-headed. They saw things all black and white—right or wrong. When you got to be Flynn's age, you began to realize that most things were in between—a shade of gray, and not necessarily Confederate gray.

* * *

FLYNN REALIZED that he didn't know as much about this feud between the two brothers as he would have liked. Personally, he had always gotten along with his brothers, though they were now separated by oceans and continents—but that was the Irish for you, spread like the windblown seeds from a wild thistle.

So he decided to find out more about this feud between young Jay and his brother. Breaking the silence, he said, "Tell me something about this young lady. She must have been something for two brothers to go fighting over her."

"Her name is Olivia. We grew up with her, really. Our families are friends. Unfortunately, she made it clear that she saw me more as a brother—a younger one."

"But she saw your brother differently, I take it."

"It didn't start out that way. The two of us were courting. We had such a good time. Olivia can make anyone laugh, and she has the best voice of anyone when we're singing."

"Singing those Rebel songs, you mean? *The despot's heel is on thy shore, Maryland, My Maryland!* Now, that's a lovely courting song, wouldn't you say?"

"No, not that one. Mostly, *Old Dog Tray* and *Come into the Garden, Maude.*"

"Singing, laughing. Lad, it sounds like things were going well. What happened?"

"Then Sid swooped in. We were all at a party, and it seemed as if he finally noticed her for the first time. Sid was always working and never had much time for parties. Anyhow, she noticed him. After that, I was second fiddle."

"Your brother, what's he like?"

"Sid? Well, he's older by five years, for a start. He's very interested in business, and no wonder—my father has already made it clear that Sid will be the one to run the family business someday."

"Which is?"

"Farming, milling, like that. Sid can go on about it for hours."

"And your father sees him as the one to run things? Imagine that. Maybe your Miss Olivia sees that as well."

"She doesn't care about money."

Flynn chuckled. He had rarely met a woman of any age who didn't care about money. He wondered how well Jay actually knew his beau. "Have you bedded her yet?"

"What? For God's sake, no!"

"So you've decided to hate your brother and run away to join the Confederate army, all for a girl who sat on the porch with you and drank lemonade?"

"What's wrong with that?"

Flynn sighed. "You don't know what you don't know, lad. There is such a thing as passion. From the sounds of it, I wouldn't be surprised if your brother Sid and this Miss Olivia know all about that. Have you bedded any girl yet?"

"Uh," Jay sputtered in embarrassment, making Flynn smile. "What do you take me for?"

"A right virgin you are. We'll fix that when we get to Richmond. I'd hate to see you killed in battle before you've known a woman. Anyhow, after that, you can decide if your Miss Olivia is still worth it."

Jay had turned red as a rooster's comb, but he managed to ask, "Still worth what?"

"This fool's errand that you're on to join the Confederacy."

"I'm not on a fool's errand!"

Flynn thought about his own errand, which was to bring back a stranger from Richmond who might or might not wish to be brought home. "You're right, lad. My apologies. I should say, the fool's errands that we're both on."

* * *

TROUBLE FOUND them on the second day.

They had made camp among a pleasant grove of trees, set back some distance from the main road. They were now deep into Virginia, in what was now Confederate territory. A brand-new country, Flynn had to remind himself. In the new Confederacy, each state was like a sovereign nation unto itself, and there were few states more powerful than Virginia. After all, Virginia's history stretched back to the founding of Jamestown in 1608, making it the very oldest of the states that had once made up the Union.

But none of that history concerned Flynn at the moment. He was more interested in breakfast. He made a breakfast from the provisions that he had brought, including some bread that was not quite stale yet, and salt pork. He also built a fire and made coffee.

"I've never tasted anything so good," Jay said, after he had devoured the food. He sat beside the fire, which was just enough to dispel the coolness of the spring morning, sipping the hot coffee from a tin mug.

"Coffee always tastes better on a morning in the outdoors," Flynn replied. "I've lived rough a few times and believe me that you never want to forget your blankets or your coffee pot."

"Sounds about right to me," Jay said.

"Glad to hear it. That means you can clean up."

Jay didn't argue, but went to rinse off the dishes in a nearby creek. He wiped them dry and stowed them in the saddlebag. Flynn watched approvingly. For someone who had grown up in a big house with servants to do all the cooking and cleaning, Jay had caught on quickly to his new reality. He seemed to be treating it all as part of the adventure.

They saddled up and rode on, neither of them feeling compelled to break the morning silence. With any luck, Flynn thought, they might reach the outskirts of Richmond by late afternoon.

The miles passed and they barely saw another soul other than field hands tending the crops. When they came to an open field, the winding road began to climb and they could see some distance behind them. Out of habit, Flynn checked their back trail.

That's when Flynn spotted the riders. They had the look of military troops about them, all wearing kepi hats rather than the broad-brimmed hats typical of the Virginia countryside. The men also appeared to have sabers. He counted a dozen men, some sort of patrol. They would be out looking for Yankees—or spies.

The sight of the patrol wasn't unexpected and might not have been cause for concern. However, as Flynn and Jay rode out into the open on the hillside, he saw the patrol in the distance stop. Someone pointed, and then the six men put spurs to their horses and began riding hell-bent for leather in their direction.

"Damn it all," Flynn said, cursing their bad luck at being spotted. A dozen men was far more than he wanted to take on by himself. He didn't plan on counting on Jay in a fight.

"What?" Jay still hadn't spotted the riders.

"Look behind us," Flynn said. "I think someone wants to know what we're up to."

"What should we do?" Jay asked. "Should we see what they want?"

"No, lad, that would be a bad idea."

"Our horses are fresh. Let's see if we can outrun them."

"That would be an even worse idea," Flynn said.

"I thought you wanted to get away?"

"What does a dog do when it sees a rabbit running away?"

"The dog chases the rabbit. Can't help it."

"That's right, lad. If you run, someone will chase you. What we'll do is keep riding and try to lose them."

Flynn nudged his horse faster without coming to an outright trot. They went up the hill and around a bend in the road, putting them out of sight of the riders, who were coming on fast. Flynn turned his horse toward the trees.

"Into the woods!"

They crashed into a stand of oaks and chestnuts. Branches battered and clawed at them, but Flynn surged deeper into the woods. A sapling whipped across his face, but Flynn held back his curse between gritted teeth. Any sound might give them away.

On the other side of the trees, he could hear hoofbeats on the road.

"Here they come!" Jay cried.

"Hush, lad. Wait for them to go by us."

They heard the patrol pounding past. Flynn felt relieved that he and Jay hadn't been spotted slipping into the woods. But the riders might not be fooled for long. If they backtracked, it wouldn't take much effort to find where they had gone off the road. The trampled grass would be a telltale sign.

"Come on," Flynn said, riding deeper into the woods. Closer to the road, the undergrowth had been thicker. Deeper in the woods, there was less underbrush and the going was easier. Soon, Flynn came to what he had been hoping for, which was a game trail. It wandered every which way and they had to duck under occasional low branches, but at least it headed away from the road. Flynn was not a natural horseman. He much preferred being on his own two feet. Jay rode more easily, ducking under the branches and guiding his horse with skill. Flynn had to admit that he was impressed. Then again, it almost went without saying that a young country gentleman would be a skilled rider. Following the trail downhill, they splashed across a stream.

From the woods above, they heard a shout.

"We've been spotted," Jay said.

"No, but they figured out where we went off the road. Come on."

There was the sound of riders crashing through the trees. They could hear the riders shouting to one another. Flynn and Jay kept riding, following the trail. In places, the tree limbs were so low that Flynn had to press himself against the horse's neck. Fallen logs littered the path from some long-ago storm, but the sure-footed horse picked his way between them. After a few minutes, the noises behind them faded.

"I think we've lost them," Jay said. He sounded more excited than concerned. It all seemed to be a big game to him.

Flynn knew the situation was more serious. Had they simply caught the attention of the patrol, or was someone actively looking for them? "We've lost them for now. We'll have to keep off the road for a while and ride cross country."

They followed the trail until it widened into a field that was green with new corn. The fields here in Virginia were certainly rich with crops. Flynn supposed that boded well for feeding an army. In the distance, they could see a barn and in the field itself, a trio of slaves paused in their work, leaned on their hoes, and stared with curiosity at the two riders who had emerged from the woods.

The bucolic scene was broken when a group of riders appeared from around the far side of the woods, galloping right at them.

"Flynn!"

"I see them, lad. They know this country better than we do, that's for sure. They must have sent riders around those woods to catch us when we came out the other side. Outfoxed, we were."

Flynn began to haul on the reins, turning the bay roan to flee, but they heard the crack of a pistol. A ball sang through the air, but well over their heads. It was a warning shot. Even so, he and the lad might have run for it, if at that moment, the riders that they had evaded in the woods now emerged from the trees.

Flynn relaxed his grip on the reins. Following his example, Jay also brought his horse to a standstill.

They were well and truly trapped.

CHAPTER SIX

Flynn spotted Jay reaching into his pocket for his derringer.

"Steady, lad," Flynn said. "That wouldn't be a good idea. We can't fight them off with that pea shooter. They'll shoot us both down like dogs."

"You have your revolver."

"Too many of them."

"Then what should we do?"

"Just let me do the talking and keep your hands where they can see them."

Flynn looked to their right and left, but there was no hope of escape. The soldiers seemed to know their business and there was no way to outride them. He feared that their trip to Richmond was going to end in this field at the end of a rope—or maybe with a bullet. On the other side of the field, he noticed that the farmhands had disappeared, as if they knew better than be a witness to what happened next.

The loose circle of riders drew closer like the loop of a drawstring tightening. He saw that they wore uniforms, the first Confederate cavalry that he had seen. Gray tunics and trousers, kepi hats, pistols in one hand, reins in the other, and sabers dangling at their sides. Flynn thought that the kepi hats were impractical compared to broad-brimmed hats, but all in all, French uniforms had provided a strong influence on military fashion. Even here in the Virginia countryside, everyone wanted to be Napoleon.

He had to admit that they were an impressive sight, from their riding boots to their well-fed horses that they maneuvered with skill. Back in Washington City, he hadn't seen any Yankee cavalry that could compare to these Confederates. He'd already heard the bragging that one Confederate cavalryman was worth ten Yankees. Maybe there was some truth to that.

"Who are you and what's your business?" asked a man with officer's insignia embroidered on the sleeves of his coat

"They were trying to give us the slip, Captain Blaine," shouted a trooper. "They must be spies! We ought to hang them."

"That's enough, Sergeant Creighton." Captain Blaine rode closer. From beneath the leather brim of his kepi hat, his dark eyes looked Flynn up and down as if judging how much rope it would take to hang him. "Is that right? Are you spies?"

"No, sir. Far from it. We came from Maryland and we're on our way to Richmond to sign up."

"Is that right? Then why did you try to hide from us? Be careful how you answer—what you say next could get you hanged."

"Not spies, sir," Flynn repeated. "We're just two riders making our way to Richmond. When we saw your patrol, we thought it would be better to stay out of your way. Less questions to answer that way."

Captain Blaine did not look convinced. Over the officer's shoulder, Flynn could see that the sergeant had reached for a coil of rope hanging from his saddle. He seemed to be keeping the rope handy for occasions such as this one and judging from the worn appearance of the rope, he had used it before.

"What's your name, anyhow?"

"Thomas Flynn."

"I thought so. You sounded Irish." From the tone of his voice, it was plain that the captain did not think highly of the Irish. Flynn was glad, however, that his name hadn't rung any bells. It was hard to know whether Rose Greenhow's errand boy would be welcome in Virginia.

Behind the captain, the sergeant had walked his horse to the edge of the woods, where he seemed to be looking for a suitable tree limb. He found one, a big oak standing a little way into the field.

"Irish, it's true, but I've lived in Richmond from time to time." Flynn didn't like how this was going. The captain and his men seemed determined that anyone they came across must be spies.

Flynn eased his hand toward the LeMat revolver, thinking that, if nothing else, he would take one or two of these Johnny Rebs to hell with him. Maybe Jay would even get off a lucky shot with that derringer.

Blaine didn't seem interested in what Flynn had to say, but turned to watch the sergeant, and nodded approvingly as the man threw the rope up and over a tree limb growing horizontal to the ground.

When Blaine turned around again, he looked at Jay and asked, "What's your story, son? Are you going to crow about not being spies, or are you going to do the honorable thing and admit it?"

To Flynn's surprise, Jay boldly moved his horse a step or two toward Captain Blaine, driving the officer back, and holding himself straight in the saddle. He looked every bit the young country gentleman.

Some of the riders leveled their pistols at him, but Jay ignored them and said, "I'm Jay Warfield, nephew of Senator Warfield of Maryland. You won't find a bigger friend to the Confederacy. This is a poor welcome for two men who want to join the Confederacy."

Flynn stared. This was the first time that he had heard this business about Senator Warfield.

Captain Blaine had changed his tune. "Warfield? I've heard of the Warfields. Why, it's one of the oldest families around Baltimore."

"One and the same," Jay said.

"Is the Irishman your servant?"

"Captain Flynn is a veteran of the Papal Wars in Italy. He served as an officer in the Battalion of St. Patrick, under Major Myles O'Reilly, and fought at the Battle of Castelfidardo."

"Is that so?" Blaine had been so sure of things a moment ago, convinced that he had caught two spies. Now, he almost looked disappointed. He gave a small shake of his head to the sergeant, who began retrieving the rope from the tree.

"If you need men, maybe we could join up with you," Jay said.

Thinking it over, Captain Blaine nodded. "That would be up to the colonel. You see, we're part of Devere's Legion. Colonel Devere recruited the entire company and paid for it out of his own pocket. I can see you have some good horses there. Judging by how you two tried to dodge us, you can definitely ride. I'm sure that we could use you."

"Then let's go see Colonel Devere," Jay said. "I hope that he can use two new officers."

Nearby, the sergeant snorted.

But Captain Blaine nodded. "Let's go see what Colonel Devere says. But first, hand over that pistol of yours, Flynn."

Flynn didn't see how he had any choice. Reluctantly, he gave the LeMat to Blaine. Jay didn't mention the pepperbox in his pocket, and neither did Flynn. "Are we prisoners?"

"Let's just say that we ain't taking any chances."

* * *

As it turned out, they were only about ten miles outside Richmond and soon reached the outskirts. Flynn had usually taken the train to Richmond and was not familiar with the road. The few times that he had traveled this way on horseback, it had usually been at night, sometimes dodging worse characters than these Confederates.

The Confederate troopers made no effort to join them in conversation. The jury still seemed to be out in their minds as to whether or not they were spies. At the same time, the riders kept them hemmed in without any hope of escape.

When he had a chance to ride close to Jay, he asked quietly, "What's this business about Senator Warfield? You never told me any of that, lad."

"*State* senator," Jay said quietly. "At least, he was until the Yankees locked him up in Fort McHenry with the rest of the secessionists. Who knows when they'll let him out?"

"I think the word *senator* was enough to impress Captain Blaine," Flynn said. "Thank you for the promotion, by the way. I was just a private in the Battalion of St. Patrick."

"I don't think that would have impressed Captain Blaine," Jay said. "Besides, this is America. You can be anything that you want to be, Captain Flynn."

They rode on to a large, rambling farmhouse that apparently served as the quarters for Devere's Legion. A few of the outbuildings had been taken over by the officers and noncommissioned officers, with the soldiers living in tents spread around the house. This was no stately plantation, but a more modest working farm, but with its large trees and green pastures, the setting was almost like a park. Remembering the conditions that he had endured in Italy, he thought that this war looked like a picnic in comparison.

Across the acreage, several members of the company were hard at work learning to be cavalry troopers. Saber drill was taking place in a field, with troopers on horseback charging past a post wrapped in burlap, whacking it with their swords as they raced by. A handful of cavalrymen fenced on horseback, the clash of their ringing swords carrying to Flynn's ears. Another group shot at targets while mounted. Yet more troopers seemed to be caught up in an exercise that involved little more than riding as fast as possible, whooping all the time. Again, this was a far cry from the military camps that Flynn recalled.

The captain had stated that Colonel Devere had paid for outfitting the company right down to the spurs and bullets, hence the name, "Devere's Legion." Flynn thought that this Devere must have deep pockets. It hadn't been an unusual practice for prominent men on both sides to set up their own units and put themselves in charge. Flynn had the thought that if only Devere been even richer, maybe he could have outfitted an entire regiment and made himself a general.

They dismounted under the shade of the trees near the front porch. He gave the flank of the bay roan a reassuring pat, hoping that it wouldn't be the last time that he saw the horse.

"Let's go see Colonel Devere," Blaine said. "Sergeant, keep that rope handy. Depending on what the colonel says, we might still need it yet."

Flynn didn't like the sounds of that, but they had no choice but to follow Blaine into the spacious farmhouse. Sergeant Creighton and a trooper followed behind, their hands not far from their pistols.

The farmhouse had a set of wide stairs leading to the second floor, with a parlor to the left. The windows were open, carrying in the spring breeze, but the house smelled of cellar damp, horses, and tobacco smoke—with a little whiskey mixed in.

In the parlor, three men stood around a table that was serving as a desk. A map was spread out on the desk, its edges held down by whiskey glasses and coffee cups. Flynn picked out the colonel right away. He was the tallest and the oldest, plus he wore the uniform with the most gold embroidery on the sleeves—more of the insignia known as "chicken guts."

"What's this?" Devere demanded, apparently annoyed by the intrusion.

Captain Blaine saluted. "Sir, these two men say they want to join up."

"Men? Captain, I see one man and a boy."

"Sir, I was concerned that they might be spies, but they claim otherwise."

"We're not spies," Flynn said.

"Who are you?"

"Captain Thomas Flynn."

"Captain? I don't see a uniform."

"I served in the Brigade of St. Patrick in Italy, sir."

"The Italian wars." Devere nodded. "Most of their officers have joined the Union, from what I hear."

"Their mistake, I'm sure."

Devere gave Flynn a piercing gaze, looking him over. Finally, he nodded. Next, he turned his attention to Jay. "Who are you, boy?"

"Jay Warfield, sir."

"Senator Warfield's nephew," the captain added. "Of the Maryland

Warfields. They have their own horses, and they appear to be good riders."

"All right," Devere said. "I don't take just anyone into my legion, but Captain Blaine seems suitably impressed. I'll give you a chance, Flynn. We could use an experienced officer, but we have enough captains as it is. I can make you a lieutenant."

"Yes, sir." Flynn still considered that to be a considerable improvement over his last rank. He hadn't intended to sign on as a soldier, but he saw now that he and Jay had little choice. If they hemmed and hawed, Sergeant Creighton was waiting on the porch with his rope, ready to hang them as spies.

Blaine was scowling at Flynn. Apparently, he wasn't pleased with the ideas of an Irishman as an officer, even if Blaine still outranked him. His glare continued as he handed back Flynn's revolver.

Devere turned his attention to Jay. "You're too wet behind the ears to be an officer, son, but I can see that making you a private won't do." Colonel Devere rubbed his chin. "I know—we'll make you a subaltern. It's not really a rank, mind you, but more like an officer in training. You can report to Lieutenant Flynn."

"Yes, sir!"

"Captain Blaine, will you do the honors?"

Blaine stepped forward. "Raise your right hand," he said.

They did as they were told, then repeated the oath that Blaine gave them:

I, Thomas Flynn, do solemnly swear or affirm that while I continue in the service I will bear true faith, and yield obedience to the Confederate States of America, and that I will serve them honestly and faithfully against their enemies, and that I will observe and obey the orders of the President of the Confederate States, and the orders of the Officers appointed over me, according to the Rules and Articles of War.

Their oath finished, Jay turned to look at Flynn, grinning from ear to ear. He had gotten what he had hoped for by coming South. He was now going to fight for the Confederacy.

Flynn's own face was grim. He had sworn allegiance to the Pope once before, and now he had taken an oath to defend Jeff Davis. Flynn hadn't planned on joining the Confederate cavalry, much less as an officer. But it beat the alternative, which might have involved a long rope and a short drop.

He was now a soldier again and like it or not, he had chosen a side. Or maybe it was better to say that one had been chosen for him.

CHAPTER SEVEN

DEVERE'S LEGION WAS NOT FOR SHOWING OFF FANCY UNIFORMS. The legion's cavalry troopers were being trained and outfitted with deadly intent. The Southerners tended to be natural-born cavalrymen, having grown up riding and shooting. They hadn't chased Yankees, but they had hunted foxes and runaway slaves across the countryside in all sorts of weather and terrain, making them familiar with being a part of coordinated groups of riders.

As much as Flynn had disliked the pompous colonel, he had to give Colonel Devere credit. When it came time to fight, his horsemen would be more than ready.

It also became clear that there were almost as many officers as men. Having attracted the cream of planter society, these privileged young men expected nothing less than being made officers. Many of them wore fancy uniforms embroidered with genuine gold or silver braid and broad-brimmed hats with ostrich plumes, like English cavaliers of old. That was certainly how they saw themselves. Much more modest uniforms had been found for Flynn and Jay.

"I'll say this, lad, you look the part," said Flynn, nodding with approval the first time that he saw Jay wearing his cavalry uniform. It turned out that Devere had cajoled one of the other young officers into providing Jay with his spare uniform. It was not as fancy as some, but it fit Jay well, right down to the stylish kepi hat. Devere had also supplied Jay with a revolver, and both men with cavalry sabers. Jay wore his sword everywhere, but Flynn thought it was a useless and clumsy thing compared to his LeMat revolver. In a fight, he much preferred to depend on a bullet than a blade. Flynn had learned to use a sword in Italy, but his principal tactic was to swing it like a giant meat cleaver.

Jay squinted at Flynn. "Where did you get that, uh, uniform?"

"What do you mean by that? I think I cut a dashing figure, wouldn't you say?"

Finding a uniform that fit Flynn had been more challenging, considering that he was bigger than most of the lithe young cavalry-men. It turned out that an unfashionable but vaguely grayish coat was secured from a fat local preacher. Brass buttons were added to give the coat a vaguely military appearance, but shortcuts were taken elsewhere.

"Nobody is going to confuse you with a Yankee, that's for sure. But are those stripes *painted* on the sleeves?"

"The men still salute me, so that's something. Then again, there are so many officers that you'd think their arms would be worn out by now."

* * *

Flynn did not much care if he was saluted or not, but for others, it was a matter of grave importance.

Just the other morning, he had seen what happened when one of the enlisted cavalrymen failed to salute Captain Blaine. Blaine was coming down the front porch steps after a meeting with the colonel. Having just stepped outdoors, Blaine was just putting his broad-brimmed hat back on his head and was adjusting it so that the ostrich feather plume would have the full effect. The cavalryman passing by made the error of bumping the captain's outstretched elbow, and also failing to salute until after the collision.

"How dare you!" the captain shouted. "I'll teach you not to salute! See if I don't!"

Blaine whipped off his hat and began using it to hit the young soldier across the head and face. It was as undignified a display of military discipline as Flynn had ever seen. A sharp word would have been sufficient. Instead, the soldier could only cower as he was swatted painfully with the heavy felt hat, until Blaine was satisfied that he'd made his point. The captain returned the hat to his head, but now the ostrich feather was badly *hors de combat*, its broken quill dangling.

By noontime, Captain Blaine's hat sported a new ostrich plume in a shade of red that was even gaudier than the last one.

"Look at that," Jay remarked. "He got himself a new feather."

"I'll bet he's got a trunk filled with 'em," Flynn said.

* * *

THIS EARLY IN THE WAR, many units on both sides were still electing their officers. Although Flynn appreciated the democratic intent, the great flaw was that officers were the result of a popularity contest. Men didn't become popular by enforcing rules and drilling their men hard. Thus, a unit that elected its officers was usually one that lacked discipline and training. To make matters worse, many of the commanding officers of these units were political appointees without any actual military skills.

Devere had avoided the issue by personally appointing all of his officers. Of course, he could do what he wanted, considering that he had funded the entire company. Wealth had its privileges and Richmond was only too glad to welcome units that were essentially small, private militias.

Like Flynn and Jay, the officers in Devere's Legion weren't actually in charge of anything other than themselves. It was Devere himself, along with Captain Blaine and Sergeant Creighton, who ran the company.

Of course, Flynn hadn't intended to become a soldier at all, but to find Anna Carroll in Richmond and convince her to return to her old friend in Washington City, Rose Greenhow. But he had been given little choice in the matter. For now, his mission would have to wait until he obtained a pass to visit the city. With any luck, this Miss Carroll would have come to her senses before then and fled the Confederacy.

* * *

Now that they were properly outfitted, Flynn and Jay joined the company for the daily drills. This generally involved using their pistols to shoot at targets from horseback, or riding their horses through a course of obstacles, all under the watchful eye of Captain Blaine or Colonel Devere.

Flynn was a decent shot with the revolver, even from the back of the horse. Riding was not his strength, however.

This morning, they found themselves playing war against other groups of riders, swinging wooden practice swords.

Flynn felt silly wielding the wooden stick, like a boy playing pirate. Also, it didn't help that he was clumsy on horseback. Flynn was big; his horse was bigger. If he had been wearing armor and armed with a lance, he would have made a formidable knight, but he was a few centuries late for that sort of war.

On the other hand, Jay was more than adept at the drill. He and the horse moved as one, dodging under a blow and thrusting at his opponent. The other rider couldn't keep himself from yelping in pain. Fortunately, the blunted wooden swords weren't heavy enough to cause real harm, but they did hurt.

Watching, Captain Blaine gave a grudging nod of approval. Young Jay Warfield was just the sort of cavalryman that Devere's Legion wanted, but in Blaine's mind, the young man was tainted by his association with Flynn. It was more than clear, from the frown that came to his face whenever he saw Flynn, that the captain had taken a dislike to Flynn. Maybe he didn't like Irishmen. That was common enough. Or maybe, deep down, he worried that Flynn had already experienced battle and Captain Blaine had not.

At the moment, Flynn had more immediate concerns. The field seemed to be filled with horsemen flying at one another, waving their

wooden swords. Flynn picked out an opposing rider who seemed a
likely victim. He swung his stick, but the other man parried, leaving
the two of them staring at each other.

"Riposte!" screamed an exasperated Captain Blaine. "For the love
of God, riposte!"

Half-heartedly, Flynn swung his sword again. His opponent parried
again, again leaving the two men at a standstill. In an actual battle, this
was the point where Flynn would have been reaching for his pistol.

He heard a horse pounding up behind him, and then a stinging
blow across his back. He turned to glare at Captain Blaine, who
wheeled his horse, ready to hit Flynn again.

"Defend yourself! Do you think that the Yankees will give you any
warning, you Irish fool!"

If Blaine was trying to provoke him, it worked. Flynn swung his
sword, but Blaine neatly stepped his horse away, then came in and hit
Flynn again while he was off balance. The wooden blade cracked
painfully against his shoulder.

"There, you would have lost an arm!" Blaine shouted triumphantly.
"Should we try for the other arm as well?"

By now, some of the other horsemen had stopped their drills to
watch the fight taking place between Blaine and Flynn. Sergeant
Creighton looked on, a nasty smile on his face.

Captain Blaine and his horse moved gracefully around Flynn, who
couldn't seem to get his horse to turn quickly enough.

Once again, Blaine rode close, his surefooted horse moving like a
four-footed dancer. He feinted, then smashed Flynn across the face
with the flat of the sword.

Blood flowed from Flynn's nose and his eyes watered, but he
ignored the pain. He shook his head to clear his vision. He had
learned a trick or two in the boxing ring. Sometimes, you had to fight
dirty.

Ignoring swordplay for the moment, Flynn drove the big bay roan
right up against the captain's horse, causing the smaller animal to
stumble. While Blaine fought to keep his balance in the saddle, the
two men were suddenly knee to knee and the captain had no room to
swing his sword. With his free hand, Flynn grabbed a handful of

Blaine's uniform coat, hauled him out of the saddle, and threw him to the ground in a heap.

Some of the men might have laughed at the sight if the fight between the two men had not taken such a serious turn—Captain Blaine was not always the most popular officer in the legion. However, he was Colonel Devere's right-hand man, and no one dared to laugh at the legion's second-in-command.

Nearby, Jay shot him a horrified glance, as if to ask, *What have you done?*

But Flynn wasn't finished. He dismounted and walked toward Blaine, the wooden sword balanced easily over his shoulder—for now. On the way, he picked up the practice sword that Blaine had dropped.

Out of the corner of his eye, Flynn saw Creighton nudge his own horse forward.

"Keep out of it, Sergeant," Flynn growled. Creighton hesitated, but it was all the time that Flynn needed.

As the captain's nimble chestnut mare trotted off and found a patch of grass to graze, Blaine managed to get to his hands and knees. The fall had knocked the wind out of him. Flynn gave him a moment to get to his feet. That wouldn't have happened in a real fight—but this was a practice field, and there were Virginia gentlemen present.

He tossed Blaine his sword. The poor man barely caught it—the fall from the horse had left him dazed.

"Do you yield?" Flynn asked. He supposed that it was what a gentleman would ask.

"What?" Blaine looked puzzled. Then he seemed to realize that he held a wooden sword in his hand. He raised it to an *en garde* position. "Hell no!"

Flynn planted his feet and hammered the sword away with such force that Blaine lost his balance and stumbled again.

"Riposte," Flynn said helpfully.

Blaine recovered and held up his sword. There was no doubt that Blaine was a good swordsman, even with a wooden blade, but he made the error of losing his temper and rushing at his opponent. Flynn stepped out of the way and managed to trip Blaine as he went past, sending the captain sprawling.

Flynn realized it was time to end this while at least one of them still had his dignity. This time, he didn't give the captain time to get up. He stepped over Blaine and gave him a good whack across the backside. The man howled through gritted teeth.

"What's that? Do you yield?"

"Go to hell, damn you!"

Flynn drew back the sword to give him another good whack. He planned to beat him like a dog, Virginia gentlemen's rules be damned.

Before Flynn could bring the sword down, a pistol shot cracked.

"Stop this at once!"

Colonel Devere came riding up, looking none too pleased with the sight of his second-in-command about to be paddled like a schoolboy. He had fired the pistol into the air to get everyone's attention.

Reluctantly, Flynn lowered the wooden sword. The colonel still held the pistol in his hand and Flynn was suddenly worried that Devere might shoot him. For a man like the colonel, there would likely be no consequences.

Devere surveyed the scene, glaring at Flynn and Blaine equally, his horse moving restlessly under him. He seemed to be making up his mind about what to do. Finally, he holstered his pistol.

"I can see that you men are full of fight. All of you!" he shouted, looking around. "Full of piss and vinegar!"

The men grinned, nodding approvingly. Coming from the colonel, this was high praise. "Yes, sir!" an eager cavalryman shouted.

"The problem is that we need to pour that piss and vinegar on the Yankees," he said. "Not on each other. We've been drilling too long. Maybe too much. Tomorrow, we'll ride out and teach some of these Yankees a lesson. I know it's what you've been waiting for!"

Cavalrymen filled the air with whooping and shouts. Some tossed their hats in the air.

"That's enough drilling for today. Get some rest, boys—after you sharpen your swords. We ride at dawn."

Flynn had to give Colonel Devere credit. It was quite a pretty little speech in more ways than one. Instead of chastising his troopers, he had managed to rouse their spirits. He had been able to blame hot tempers on the Yankees, rather than find fault with his officers—or more importantly, his second in command.

Expertly, Devere wheeled his horse and rode back toward his head-quarters in the farmhouse.

Flynn glanced at Captain Blaine. Neither man offered to shake hands. The captain glared at him with open hostility before turning away to find his chestnut mare.

"You sure poked the hornet's nest," Jay said, suddenly appearing at Flynn's side. "I thought you were going to kill him. You seem like you still might do just that."

"Not if he kills me first, lad."

Flynn knew the expression on Captain Blaine's face all too well. He had seen it across card tables and boxing rings. He had seen it across the battlefield as well. It was a look of pure hatred.

If Blaine hadn't liked him before, things were now much worse. Flynn now had a mortal enemy.

CHAPTER EIGHT

ANNA ELLA CARROLL WANDERED THE STREETS IN THE VICINITY OF the Virginia State Capitol building in Richmond, which was where the 257 members of the Confederate Congress were currently meeting. She was dressed respectably, marking her as a woman of means, though not fashionable or flashy, and several ladies and men offered a polite nod as they passed by, even when she did not know them. The Confederate city was small enough that they knew *her*, if only by reputation.

Also, Richmond society was nothing if not polite, although she suspected that its citizens would not be as welcoming if they knew her true purpose, which was to do her part to bring the Confederacy to a quick end and thus preserve the Union.

"Ma'am," said a passing officer, tipping his hat.

"Major," she replied, seeing that the man was pleased that she had recognized his rank.

No wonder—these last few days, she had become a student of the Confederate military. She could easily tell a major from a colonel, and an infantryman from a horse soldier.

As she made her way from East Cary Street to Main Street, the sense of excitement in the air was palpable. After all, this was the founding of a new nation, however misguided that founding might be.

She had the thought that Richmond must have had an atmosphere similar to the one in Philadelphia, back in the heady first days of Independence—or at least, the days before General Howe had marched up from the Chesapeake Bay with thousands of Redcoats and occupied the city.

She wondered how long it would take Union troops to do much the same. In her own way, Anna was determined to do whatever she could to help that process along.

"Good morning, Miss Carroll," said a passing government official. She recognized him as Henry Porter, a deputy to one of Jefferson Davis's cabinet secretaries, who maintained an office near the Capitol.

"Good morning to you as well," Anna said, navigating to block his path and thus force the man to slow down enough to engage him in conversation. She knew that he oversaw wartime production in several factories. Textiles, wasn't it? Or something to do with foundries?

Finding his way blocked by her hoop skirts, Porter had no choice but to stop. But he had been in a hurry and now seemed flustered. "May I help you, Miss Carroll?"

"I just wanted to thank you for what you are doing. It takes a certain expertise to manage, well ..."

"The ironworks," he said, no longer looking as exasperated. Like many civilian managers, he was all too glad when anyone expressed interest in his work. The military officers were the ones who got all the glory.

She nodded toward the Capitol building, where crowds were already gathering, and said, "It looks as if you are going to have another busy day, sir."

"It would appear that way," he said. "We'll let the politicians argue it out. My business is making sure that the troops are well supplied."

"I am sure that you have your duties well in hand, Mr. Porter. How is production going?" she asked.

"Why, very well," he said, warming to the topic. He seemed to have forgotten that he was in a hurry to go anywhere. "We have the Tredegar Ironworks running around the clock. Our only limitation is getting enough iron ore in to supply the furnaces. Of course, our sources from western Maryland have been cut off and we have to rely on what can be found within our new nation."

"I'm sure that's challenging," Anna said. "Is the Richmond and Petersburg Railroad bringing in ore from the Blue Ridge?"

"Why, yes. You do know your geography, Miss Carroll! The Cloverdale and Grace mines are some of our best sources to supply the ironworks." Porter tipped his hat. "Speaking of which, I must attend to business. Have a good day, Miss Carroll."

She wished him the same and moved on, pleased at the conversation, having garnered another tidbit of information that she could pass along to her sources in the north. It was no secret that the Tredegar Ironworks was the South's key manufacturer of cannons for its new army and navy. The source of the iron ore might be valuable news, however.

Anna did not think of herself as a spy, which seemed a sneaking thing to be, but rather as a gatherer of information. She gathered it in just this way, picking up bits and pieces from the Confederate officials and generals that she encountered on a daily basis since her arrival in Richmond.

Her secret weapon was male vanity. Men of all ages liked to inflate their own importance, or when provoked, they felt a need to prove that they were smarter than her—usually revealing information in the process.

For example, when she had stroked Porter's ego regarding his expertise, he had been eager to oblige by readily discussing the Confederacy's main source of iron ore.

Other men required a different approach. The more sanctimonious officials and officers needed to be challenged. When she questioned their knowledge, they were quick to take the bait. It brought out the fool in them nicely.

Anna was more than happy to bring her considerable intellect to bear when the need for that tactic arose.

How long she could continue to gather information without attracting notice was anyone's guess.

* * *

FOR THE MOST PART, Anna was taken for granted and barely given a second glance. After all, Anna was neither fashionable, nor rich, nor beautiful. None of the things that attracted attention in the usual way. Instead, she was seen as a figure deserving of understanding, or possibly of pity. Anna had put about the story that she had been forced to flee to Richmond due to her secessionist views, leaving her in reduced circumstances.

Southerners did love a tragic story. What was it about the South that engendered that? They also loved their aristocracy. As the grand-daughter of Charles Carroll, a signer of the Declaration of Independence who had owned more than a thousand slaves, and the daughter of Charles King Carroll, a governor of Maryland, there were few Southerners with a pedigree as fine as hers.

Her cousins still owned Doughoregan Manor, the sprawling estate outside Baltimore that had been her grandfather's. Their slaves had long since been freed and hired on as laborers, even given land on which to live.

Her immediate family's fortunes had not been as good. It was true that father had been a brilliant scholar of the law and she had learned a great deal from him. Her status freed her from the household drudgery most young rural women faced, and instead, she spent her time devouring the books in his extensive law library. They sometimes had discussions about fine legal points that lasted for hours in his cool study that smelled pleasantly of leather-bound volumes and cigar smoke. To be sure, it was not the usual way that a young woman spent her time.

Her father had not practiced law, preferring to use his knowledge for legislative arguments at the statehouse in Annapolis. This meant relying on their plantation income. Even the word "plantation" was something of a stretch when describing the farm near Pocomoke City on Maryland's Eastern Shore. The crops were poor, with many of the fields weedy and overgrown.

In fact, by the time that Anna was a young woman, most of the family's remaining wealth had been in the form of the slaves that they owned. Her father had known this and was uncomfortable about owning slaves, but remained reluctant to part with the last shreds of his wealth. Also, owning slaves made little sense from an economic standpoint. There was barely enough income to clothe and feed them. But in his way, her father felt responsible for the welfare of his enslaved plantation workers. These were people who had lived on this land for generations, with no other source of income. The question of slavery always loomed large in the Carroll household.

Her father was a capable politician, well-respected and level-headed, but public office paid only a small honorarium. Serving as her father's secretary, she had benefitted from connections with many of the leading citizens of Maryland and surrounding states. Behind the scenes, she had even written legislation and campaign speeches for her father, Governor Hicks, and the presidential campaign of Millard Fillmore. Of course, as a woman, her name never appeared anywhere.

Bills have a way of coming due. Once her father retired from public office, he seemed even less interested in any financial matters and left them to his daughter.

To avert fiscal disaster, the plantation was sold. They moved to a respectable, but much smaller property nearby.

But first, Anna emancipated the families who had been enslaved by the Carrolls for generations.

She might have married her way into money, but that didn't appeal to Anna. Plain and outspoken, she managed to turn away the few men who expressed an interest in her.

Anna had been forced to turn the family home into a finishing school for young women. She detested the idea of teaching young ladies how to curtsy, set a table, or dress. The girls were mostly vapid and empty-headed daughters of the local gentry.

She yearned for a return to politics. In a most unlikely way, that chance came with the election of Abraham Lincoln. At first glance, a former slave owner and member of the old Maryland aristocracy appeared to be an unlikely supporter of the Republican party and the likes of Abraham Lincoln, who was nothing more than a frontier upstart, after all.

However, Anna had felt the winds of war tug at her mind. The republic that her family had worked so hard to create was in danger. She became a staunch Unionist.

Anna turned her powerful pen to supporting the Union. Soon, she was a familiar figure in Washington City, even at the White House itself. She wrote convincing political pamphlets. Lincoln seemed amused by her, but he listened to her opinions. If she had been a man, there was no doubt that she would have been an appointee to an important office or even been a cabinet member.

Instead, shunned by the men who ran the government, here she was in Richmond, doing what she could. She sometimes felt bitter about it, but she was determined to do what she could to help the Union. Perhaps, in the end, someone might recognize her contributions.

If Anna had been a different person, she might have turned her back on the ungrateful people in Washington City and started a new life here. She could have secured a husband for herself in the Confederate capital, perhaps one of the older Confederate officers—not someone who would expect a younger, richer wife, but maybe an aging colonel or brigadier general who admired her pedigree and would not be too demanding.

But that was not Anna. She saw marriage as another form of slavery—one for women. Once married, women were considered nothing more than the property of their husbands.

She could do better, indeed. She could be the master of herself.

If she helped preserve the Union in the process, so much the better.

* * *

ANNA WALKED ON. This time, she encountered General Hunter. White-haired and white-bearded, he seemed glad of the attention she gave him.

"Good morning, sir," she said. "I thought you would be in the field with your troops."

"Oh, I will be soon enough," Hunter said. "We will be riding out to teach those Yankees a lesson."

"I certainly hope so," Anna said, then decided to goad him. "People are beginning to talk, wondering why our troops do nothing."

"Who would say such things?" The old general demanded, a bit of fire showing in his eyes. "Why, they don't know what they're talking about. This very morning we are making plans. Plans, I tell you, for an invasion of the north. We have General Johnston going up through the Shenandoah Valley while General Beauregard attacks Washington itself. It is a perfect pincher movement, you see, coming at them from two directions, like a hammer and an anvil."

He punched his gloved fist into his open hand to emphasize the point.

"Why, General Hunter. That's brilliant. I know that we will all be reassured by putting the Yankees in their place."

"Indeed, Miss Carroll." She wanted to press him for details, but the general said, "If you will excuse me, I have business to attend to."

"I am sure that you do, sir."

The general bowed and walked on.

Satisfied with her morning fact-gathering, Anna headed back to the modest, but respectable, rooming house that she occupied.

On the way, she saw troops everywhere, squads of young soldiers marching past. Cavalry rode by as if for no other purpose than to display their new uniforms and clattering swords. Some of them even wore plumes in their hats.

She did her best to keep track of the various units, their sizes, and their officers. It must all be useful to someone, somewhere, in an office in Washington City.

General Hunter had let slip that there would soon be an invasion of the north. That was important information to pass along. As was usual with most men, he had probably told her too much by revealing the names of the generals who would lead the campaign against the Union, from two different directions. It would have been better to learn more details, but she could show only so much interest before even someone as obtuse as General Hunter became suspicious.

She reached her modest accommodations and was pleasantly surprised to find two invitations awaiting her. One was from a group of ladies who planned to make bandages.

She set that one aside, having no interest in making anything with her hands, and especially no interest in conversation with wives who failed to grasp anything of import. She also believed that the invitation smacked a little of pity for her lonely situation in Richmond. Anna needed no one's pity.

The second invitation proved more promising. It was to a party being given for the officers of Devere's Legion. She had heard of them, an elite cavalry unit recruited and outfitted by Colonel Devere, a wealthy Virginian. If anyone was going to take part in this action against Washington, it would certainly be Devere's Legion.

Perhaps once the officers had enjoyed too much punch, they would be more than happy to brag about their role in the coming expedition. Anna smiled. She would be glad to pass along those details to officials in the north. Gathering information was knitting of an altogether different sort, putting together bits and pieces to make something whole. This appealed to her far more than making bandages and knitting scarves.

Again, Anna would not have considered herself a spy, but only a gatherer of information from Confederate officials.

Whether she admitted it to herself or not, Anna Ella Carroll, scion of the Old Line State's slave-holding aristocracy, was playing a very dangerous game.

CHAPTER NINE

IN A SWIRL OF DUST AND A CLANKING OF HARNESS AND SABERS, Devere's Legion rode out. For most of the men, there was a feeling of being unleashed after long weeks of drill and training. Of course, Flynn and Jay had been cavalrymen for far less time, but even they were eager to do something besides practice with wooden swords.

There were rumors of Union raiders prowling the Virginia countryside and Devere intended to drive them off and teach them a lesson.

"We ain't just pretty faces, boys!" Devere had announced that morning, to general laughter. "We aim to fight!"

Grudgingly, Flynn had to admit that Devere had the ability to inspire his men. He certainly looked the part of a cavalry leader. And there was no doubt that Devere must have deep pockets to have funded this entire company as his own personal militia.

There were rumors that Devere had made his fortune trading cotton, or that he had been a lumber baron, or even a slave trader. The world of business was something of a mystery to Flynn, who considered it a good day if he won a pocketful of money in a card game or a boxing match, but he had known his share of self-made men. They were usually a hard-nosed lot. Devere did not seem cut from the same cloth.

Even Jay was curious about the origins of Devere's fortune. "How do you suppose Devere got all his money?"

"Oh, I suspect that Devere made his money the old-fashioned way."

"What do you mean?"

"He inherited it, that's what I mean!"

It was as good a theory as any. The question was, what would the dashing Colonel Devere be like in an actual battle? Were he and the legion just for show?

They might soon find out.

Most of the men were glad to be riding out after weeks or even months of waiting for a chance to use their swords and pistols against the enemy.

Flynn had mixed emotions as he trotted the bay roan along the road. He hadn't intended to become a soldier, yet here he was, riding out as part of the legion. He also wasn't any closer to his intended errand of finding and returning the mysterious Miss Carroll to Washington. He had yet to so much as set eyes on the woman, but his time away from the legion's training camp to look for her in Richmond had been limited. If anything, he felt that he was leaving behind his real purpose for coming south in the dust churned up by the horses' hooves.

Through the dust, Flynn still managed to admire the scenery. The countryside here was relatively flat on the outskirts of Richmond, just a stone's throw from the James River. As they rode north, gentle hills began to appear. The early summer crops flourished, corn mostly, along with fields of wheat and barley, as well as hay. It was bountiful country, to be sure.

As for this expedition to chase off the Union cavalry, Flynn didn't think that he had any choice but to go along—even if it resulted in a skirmish against Union troops. His feud with Captain Blaine meant that the man kept a sharp eye on Flynn. When Blaine himself wasn't present, it seemed as if Sergeant Creighton was there instead. If Flynn tried to slip away, he was sure that Blaine would like nothing better than to hunt him down as a deserter. The result would be a short fall from a long rope.

Also, Flynn now had Jay to worry about. If Flynn tried to desert from the legion, one way or another, Captain Blaine would surely try to implicate Jay. It would be guilt by association.

As an officer, Flynn found himself in charge of a small squad of riders. Most of the men were misfits who seemed to sense that Flynn was no more an officer than was the colonel's milk cow. They only gave him some grudging respect because they liked Captain Blaine even less.

"We're finally going to see some action. Do you think that we'll be fighting Union troops?" Jay asked, once they had paused briefly at a crossroads several miles from the farm.

"I think we'll be fighting *someone*—or chasing them," Flynn said. "It sounds as if Devere wants to make sure that our swords are blooded, one way or another."

Before riding out, Devere had assembled his officers and announced that they would be in search of Union troops, Yankee sympathizers, or outright spies. It soon became clear that Devere planned to find some quarry or get his boys into action, no matter what. They were spoiling for a dust-up, and Devere did not intend to disappoint them.

The troopers were excited, but jittery. They hadn't found their rhythm yet, despite all the drills, and kept bunching up as they rode, crowding their horses together.

"Spread out," Flynn reminded them. "We have all the space we want between here and Washington."

Grudgingly, Flynn had to admit that Captain Blaine was capable enough as an officer, though he might be petty and pompous. Blaine's worst fault, Flynn thought, was that he clearly worshipped Devere. He'd follow that man into hell and not ask questions. For now, Blaine rode at the side of the road, so that he could move at will up and down the column of cavalrymen.

The way that Flynn saw it, Devere had one objective—to make Devere look like a conquering hero. The legion was simply an extension of the man's ego.

He rode at front of column like a knight of yore, flags flying, including a banner that Flynn recognized as a coat of arms—apparently for the Devere family.

Devere might have a clear road ahead of him, but the troopers following him were not so fortunate.

No one had counted on the dust. It was a by-product that resulted from more than one hundred horses passing over roads that hadn't seen rain in two weeks, leaving them to bake in the early summer heat. The swirling cloud hovered over the column. The dust settled into their clothes, clogged their eyes, gritted between their teeth. The men swished their mouths out and spat before daring to take a drink. Some had started wearing scarves or cloths across their faces, making them look like bandits.

Devere didn't seem to have any official orders. He had set out on this mission on his own accord. Devere's decision to ride out with his legion might have been premature or even reckless, but his men didn't mind because they were more than eager for action.

The question was, would Devere be able to give them any?

* * *

BY NOONTIME, the legion had reached an area of rolling hills dotted with small farms. They were that much closer to Washington, but there was still no sign of anyone resembling a Union soldier.

From time to time, they were met by Virginians who gave them baskets of biscuits, bread and butter, even a jug of moonshine that the officers quickly seized for their own stock of supplies.

But as it turned out, not everyone was as eager to share with the cavalry.

The lead elements of the legion came across a farmer riding a horse and leading another. Devere spurred his horse toward the man.

"What's your business, sir?" Colonel Devere demanded.

The farmer did not seem cowed by the sight of so many cavalrymen. Flynn decided that he was either oblivious, or a fool.

"I'm on my way back from the neighbor's," the farmer said. "What do you care? It's still a free country, ain't it?"

"I shall ask the questions," Devere said. "Why would you need two horses to visit your neighbor?"

"Why, to see if he wanted to buy this one," the farmer said, nodding at the horse he led.

"That looks like a satisfactory horse," Devere said. "So does the horse you are riding. You can sell them to us."

"Hold on. I'm only selling the one horse."

"No matter. We need them both. The Confederacy needs them both."

"What, do you expect me to walk home?"

"I am sure it's not far. Captain Blaine, pay the man."

Blaine rode forward, offering the farmer a handful of currency.

"Why, this is Confederate scrip!" the farmer said.

"Indeed it is."

The newly independent states had rushed to create their own currency. The result was a confusing array of paper money, some issued by independent banks, some bills issued by the states, and yet more money printed by the central government. It was no wonder that more than a few viewed the Confederate currency with suspicion.

"This money ain't worth the paper it's printed on. I'll only take gold for these horses."

"You will take Confederate legal tender, or you will take lead," Colonel Devere said. "Your choice, sir."

Devere drew his pistol. He thumbed back the hammer with an audible click that made his horse's ears prick up. For a long moment, it seemed as if he might shoot the farmer.

The farmer went pale, realizing that he did not have much choice. He dismounted and reached out to accept the handful of bills that Captain Blaine offered.

"This is robbery, I tell you," the farmer complained.

"You have been paid," Blaine said, putting a hand to the butt of his pistol. "If I were you, I would accept the money and say no more."

The farmer glared, but kept his mouth shut as his horses were led away. He would have to make his way home on foot.

"Thank you for your patriotism, sir," Colonel Devere said, then spurred his horse away.

Similar scenes were repeated along the way. Horses, chickens, even green corn were considered fair game by Devere's Legion. To pay for it all, Devere seemed to have an endless supply of the Confederate money at his disposal.

Flynn began to suspect that the farmer they had encountered earlier was right to have requested payment in gold, but none of that was being paid out.

Paper money or lead—it wasn't much of a choice.

* * *

THEY RODE until early afternoon without further incident, heading steadily north. By then, the horses were winded and the men were dusty. Orders were given to camp for the night. They had reached a pleasant, shaded grove that, until lately, had been occupied by cattle. The cattle had been chased away, and the men gladly watered their horses in the stream that passed through the grove. There was an old stone springhouse in the shade of the grove, and to their delight, some of the men discovered milk and butter inside.

After seeing to his men, Flynn found himself summoned before Captain Blaine. Flynn was amused to see that the captain was just as dusty as his men. His ostrich plume now resembled a well-used feather duster. His black riding boots had started out the day gleaming with polish, but they now looked as brown and dusty as the road itself.

"Lieutenant Flynn, you will take the second watch of picket duty tonight."

"Yes, sir," Flynn said without enthusiasm. This meant that he and his men would not get a full night's sleep because it would be interrupted by the need to go on guard duty.

"Can't be too careful," the captain said. "We're so close to Washington that we may encounter Union troops at any moment."

Flynn knew that the captain had a valid point, but he couldn't help but think that Blaine had singled out his squad as a kind of punishment. "Very well, sir."

He encouraged his men to get what sleep they could, then awakened them at midnight. They kept watch for four hours while the camp slept peacefully, without any sign of Union raiders. Knowing how jumpy his men might be, perhaps even a danger to each other, he had taken the precaution of having them unload their guns.

Jay had been incredulous. "What if the Yankees attack?"

"The Yankees won't attack, lad. They like their sleep, the same as we do."

Eventually, they returned to their blankets. At best, they could hope to snatch another hour or so of sleep before reveille.

All too soon, they were roused from their slumber for another day of riding.

CHAPTER TEN

By mid-morning, they were more than twenty miles from Richmond. Flynn wondered if Devere planned to take them all the way to Washington City. In that case, there would be no shortage of Federal troops.

Flynn was nearly dozing in the saddle when he heard an excited cry.

"Cavalry!" someone shouted. "Federal cavalry!"

Sure enough, in the distance, he could see a small group of blue-coated riders. No more than a dozen men.

Flynn guessed that the Federals were doing much the same as the legion was doing—probing the enemy, scouting, and looking for action. They had found it, all right, but they were badly outnumbered by the legion.

The Federals seemed to reach the same conclusion. They turned their horses and rode away.

It soon became clear that Colonel Devere did not plan to let them go so easily. To the sound of a blowing bugle, the gray-clad riders gave chase. Several men draw their pistols and fired, the sound of the sharp cracks filling the air. At this range, they were just wasting ammunition.

That didn't stop the Union cavalry from returning fire. It turned out that they were better armed than the Confederates. To Flynn's surprise, a few bullets whistled over their heads, uncomfortably close.

"They have carbines, not just pistols," Flynn said.

"What does that mean?" Jay wondered.

"It means that this isn't a fox hunt. It's serious business. We're almost in range of those carbines. I just hope Colonel Devere knows that."

Despite the threat from the Union bullets, the entire column of gray riders raced after them, with Colonel Devere in the lead. It helped that he seemed to have the fastest horse, his coal-black stallion leading the way. Then again, most of his men seemed to know better than to outride him.

The horses left the dusty road behind and galloped pell-mell across the fields, leaping low wooden fences and trying to close the distance between them and the blue-coated raiders. The Union troops had stopped firing and scarcely looked back, riding hard.

Flynn wondered where they were going. Did they hope to outride the Confederates and lose them? They certainly could have no hope of fighting the entire legion. It seemed odd for such a small number of Union cavalrymen to be riding so deep into Virginia.

Flynn began to have the nagging suspicion that maybe they weren't alone, after all. The men they were chasing might be part of a much larger unit.

The legion might be riding into a trap.

Colonel Devere seemed to share none of these concerns.

"After them!" he shouted, urging his men on to even greater speeds. "There's not a Yankee alive who can outride a Virginian!"

It looked as if he might be right. Devere and some of the others were gaining on the Union troops. A stream appeared in the distance, and some of the blue-clad cavalry splashed across.

But not all. Three or four soldiers slid from their horses and took shelter behind logs and rocks. It was clear that they planned to fight a rear-guard action to enable the others to ford the stream and get away.

With the longer range of their carbines, some of their shots began to have a telling effect. A man riding near the head of the column suddenly threw up his hands, then fell headlong from the saddle.

Devere seemed to realize that riding on would have a heavy price. He slowed and began shouting orders. He waved Flynn over.

"Lieutenant Flynn, I want you to ride out with your squad and probe the enemy. Get as close as you can. While you do that, I'll have Captain Blaine ride around and flank them."

"Yes, sir."

Flynn couldn't find fault with the strategy. What he didn't like was that he and his men, including Jay, were being used as decoys to distract the enemy. He had tried to keep his head down since the confrontation with Captain Blaine on the training field, but it was clear that Colonel Devere had not forgotten. The colonel needed Captain Blaine, but Flynn was expendable.

He gathered his squad. Like Flynn and Jay, they were all newcomers to the legion, without strong ties to the other men. A couple of them were drunks and troublemakers—men that nobody else wanted in their squad. It made no difference. Today, they would be proving themselves under fire.

"All right, lads, our orders are to attack those Yankees and draw their fire."

"They've got a longer range than us," Jay pointed out as another bullet whined overhead. It didn't help that the Union men seemed to be crack shots with those carbines. Jay looked white-faced and shaken—not unusual at all for the first time that someone came under fire.

"Aye, that they do. That's why we're going to dismount and use whatever cover we can find while we advance." If Colonel Devere had expected a spectacular cavalry charge with drawn sabers, he was going to be disappointed. Flynn planned to attack on his own terms.

"Jay, I want you to stay back here and hold the horses."

"What? No, I'm going with the rest of you."

"Stay here, lad. That's an order."

Leaving Jay behind, Flynn moved forward with the rest of the squad. The Union troopers had also dismounted and were using logs and brush along the stream bank for cover as they fired intermittently at the legion. As Flynn watched, Captain Blaine peeled away from the main column with a group of riders. If the Yankees had noticed that, they would be keeping an eye out. It would be Flynn's job to distract them.

He raised the LeMat and fired a shot.

First time, he thought. How many more times will I shoot at someone in this war?

His bullet disappeared into the blue sky, but he hadn't been hoping to hit anything—just to make the Union troopers keep their heads down.

He fired again. Around him, the other legionnaires began to do the same.

"Use whatever cover you can find, lads," Flynn said, then sprinted several feet ahead toward a stump. For his trouble, a bullet hit the stump and sent splinters flying.

Behind him and to his left, a legionnaire named Milburn cried out and fell into a patch of weeds.

"I'm hit, boys, I'm hit!"

The man struggled to get to his feet, but another bullet passed near him.

"Stay down, you damn fool," Flynn shouted at him. "I'll come to you."

Flynn raised his pistol and fired in the direction of a patch of gun smoke, although he still wasn't in pistol range. More shots quickly followed from the Yankees. He had heard that the carbines were fast to shoot, and the rumors were true. He was starting to think that he and the others were well and truly pinned down.

Where in the hell was Captain Blaine? he wondered. Probably adjusting his ostrich plume, that's where.

That's when he heard a shout, followed by thundering hoofbeats. A dark shadow passed over the spot where Flynn crouched and with a shock, he realized that it was Jay, riding like a madman toward the Yankees.

"You fool boy," Flynn muttered. More shots cracked and Flynn fully expected to see Jay tumble from the saddle.

But Jay ducked low in the saddle and expertly wheeled his horse, racing parallel to the stream bank not more than fifty feet from where the Yankees were making their stand. The maneuver took the Yankees by surprise, their shots going wide. Jay rose up in the saddle and raised his arms wide, like he was flying. More carbines cracked. Then Jay swooped low on the far side of the saddle, offering hardly any target at all. It was brave, foolhardy, and some of the best riding that Flynn had ever seen.

He raced to Milburn's side. He'd been hit in the shoulder, but the bullet had only grazed him.

"You'll live," Flynn announced. "Now, get on your feet."

"What?"

"Do it!" Jumping up, Flynn cried "Come on, lads!"

Charging forward, they leaped over stumps and brush, right at the Yankees, who had been so riveted by Jay's display of horsemanship that Flynn and the rest of the squad managed to take them by surprise.

Closer now, Flynn fired at a trooper who was reloading. The man slumped and fell. Though wounded, Milburn managed to fire his pistol with his left hand. Another trooper dropped.

The remaining Yankees seemed to have had enough. They splashed across the stream, some of them managing to mount their horses, with others simply grabbing the reins and running alongside their horses through the water.

Finally, Captain Blaine and his men arrived, blowing bugles, shouting, and firing shots at the retreating Yankees. They made a great deal of noise, but it was clear that the enemy had already been routed. Flynn's squad had done its job, with help from Jay's spectacular riding.

Colonel Devere came riding up. "That's the way to make them run, boys! Keep that up and the war will be over before you know it!"

Several men whooped.

Captain Blaine approached, clearly pleased with himself. Even Devere was smiling from ear to ear, which was a change from his usual severe expression. "Now, that was something!" Devere said. "That was some of the best riding I've ever seen!"

Blaine's smile faded as he realized that the colonel was looking past him at Jay.

Several men echoed the colonel. "Now, that was something! You sure showed those Yankees!"

Jay quietly accepted the praise, smiling.

Flynn shook his head. The lad had proved himself, even if he was damn lucky to still be alive. As far as Flynn was concerned, it was a minor miracle that he hadn't been shot off that horse.

Looking around, Flynn could see that the only man who didn't seem happy about the praise being heaped on Jay was Captain Blaine. As Flynn watched, the captain's frown deepened.

Flynn was puzzled at first, but then it dawned on him why Captain Blaine looked so unhappy. The captain had planned on sweeping in and making a show of routing the Yankees, but the lad had stolen his thunder. It was Jay, not Captain Blaine, who was getting all the glory.

Damn it all, Flynn thought. It would be just like Captain Blaine to hold a grudge out of jealousy. One way or another, Flynn was sure that Blaine would have his revenge against young Jay.

The Union raiders had splashed to safety across the creek. Colonel Devere had let them go, giving no orders to pursue the Yankees. Apparently, Devere's Legion was not ready to invade the north just yet. Devere had given his boys a first taste of battle. His feeling seemed to be that he had blooded them and that was enough.

One of the other legionnaires had been wounded by the Union troops' long-range shooting, but he remained in the saddle. Two of the blue-coated cavalrymen—the enemy, Flynn reminded himself—had not been so lucky. They lay sprawled in the sandy soil along the stream bank. In small groups, the legionnaires came to inspect the bodies, drawn by curiosity. The dead cavalrymen wore pale blue trousers and dark blue coats, stained now with blood. Like the Confederates, they wore kepis, but theirs were blue. Both men had neatly trimmed beards and their faces had not yet begun to swell in the heat. All of that was normal enough and the Virginians were no strangers to death. It was common practice to prepare bodies for burial at home. However, the men were more used to death brought on by disease and old age. The results of violent death were something new.

For most, it was the dead Yankees' eyes that were disturbing—the dead men both had pale eyes, staring sightlessly into the summer sky.

A few of the men were less introspective. They gathered up the soldiers' weapons and took what souvenirs they could, including a few greenbacks that one of the dead men had in his pocket.

Devere did nothing to stop the looting of the dead. In fact, he claimed one of the carbines for himself.

"I wish we had a hundred of these," he said.

Jay had approached alongside Flynn, to get a look at the soldiers up close. Flynn could see that the sight of the dead men was finally making the fact that war was a serious, gruesome business sink in for the others, including Jay.

"That could have been my brother," Jay said. "For all I know, Sid could already have been killed somewhere else."

"That seems unlikely, given that there hasn't been any real fighting. Besides, I thought that seeing your brother dead would make you happy. From what you've told me, I thought you would be disappointed that you weren't the one who got to shoot him."

Jay took a while answering. "Of course I'd be disappointed," he finally said, but he didn't sound so sure.

That was the thing about war, Flynn thought. He had seen the same thing in Italy. At first, it seemed like a fine adventure, getting to wear a fancy uniform and joking with the lads. But all that changed with the first battle and the first time that you saw the dead. War reaped a bitter harvest.

"Don't worry, lad. You saw how those Yankees ran. This war might well be over before you have to shoot your brother."

"What's going to happen to them? The dead men, I mean."

Flynn nodded at two troopers approaching with shovels. "They'll get an unmarked grave on Virginia soil, that's what. Unless you want to end up like them, lad, I would suggest that you don't ride in front of the enemy like you did today. That was foolish. Also, you've upset Captain Blaine."

"Captain Blaine? What are you talking about?"

"Just stay out of his sight for a while, lad. Trust me on that. Now, unless you want to help dig these graves, let's mount up."

CHAPTER ELEVEN

THEY HAD CHASED OFF A UNION PATROL, BUT FOR DEVERE'S Legion, another challenge remained. The officers had been invited to Richmond for a grand cotillion in their honor to celebrate the Fourth of July. It seemed that both the Union and the Confederacy had laid claim to Independence Day.

"I'd rather face a firing squad," Flynn complained, when he heard the news.

"But it's a party!" Jay enthused. "What's wrong with that?"

"Parties have rules, like how to bow to the ladies and how to hold your glass of bourbon," Flynn said.

"Your punch," Jay corrected him. "The bourbon is usually *in* the punch."

"There you go," Flynn said. "See what I mean? Maybe I can stay behind."

"That woman you've been looking for might attend the party," Jay pointed out. "Anyone of importance will be there. I believe you said her name was Miss Carroll?"

Flynn put a finger to his lips and said quietly, "The less said about that, the better, lad. It would be better if Colonel Devere doesn't get wind of that."

"Sorry," Jay said. "But you don't have any choice. You're an officer now, Lieutenant Flynn. You have to go to that party."

Flynn knew that the lad was right. Refusing to attend the party might only bring him unwelcome attention, but he fretted about it all the same. It was clear that Jay and the other officers had been educated in the social graces. As much as Flynn tried to hide it, the fact was that he had begun life in an Irish cottage with a thatched roof and a dirt floor. The prospect of a moonlight and magnolias cotillion might be welcomed by others, but the notion made him feel as nervous as a long-tailed cat in a room full of rocking chairs.

Still, he polished his buttons and blacked his boots for the occasion. Many of the officers had dress uniforms, but Flynn would just have to make do with brushing down his moth-eaten gray coat.

Maybe Jay was right and he would find Miss Carroll there, meeting her at long last. If nothing else, he could get drunk—Jay had hinted that the punch contained bourbon—and maybe pick a fight if the boredom got to be too much. He had to admit that there was a lot more to being an officer than he had expected.

THE PARTY WAS BEING GIVEN at the home of a leading Richmond businessman named Lewis Ginter, who was an acquaintance of Colonel Devere's. The stately house opened up into a backyard enclosed by a brick wall and magnolia trees of various sizes, some of them so broad and tall that they must be ancient. Lantern light played off the waxy green leaves and illuminated the large white blossoms.

In addition to the legion's officers, many of the city's leading citizens seemed to be there. They were certainly well dressed, with some of the men wearing white gloves and silk hats. One elderly gentleman looked regal in a snowy suit. The women seemed to be draped in acres of silk, shaped by wide hoops. Many of the women wore curled tresses with faces smoothed out by beeswax and touched by rouge.

Flynn looked about for Miss Carroll, but none of the women seemed to match the plain face that he recalled from the *carte de visite* that Rose Greenhow had shown him back in Washington. Every woman here seemed to be a beauty and Flynn watched, mesmerized, as they flirted with the officers. He saw that Jay was trying to hold the attention of a lovely young creature in a deep green gown, but without much success. She seemed more interested in the officers a few years older than Jay, who looked boyish in comparison. Finally giving up, Jay stationed himself near the punchbowl.

"Go easy on that punch, lad," Flynn warned, having sampled the punch and found that it packed a wallop. He had seen the servants mixing it—a bottle of whiskey, a bottle of water, lemon juice, a few shakes of bitters, and a cup of sugar. The result was sweet and intoxicating. He had also noticed that no one much cared about how he held his punch glass.

"Oh, don't worry about me," Jay said. "I could drink this all night and not feel a thing."

"Just hearing you say that is what worries me."

Flynn shook his head and left the lad to his punch.

Colonel Devere held court beneath a particularly majestic magnolia. Dappled from below by the light of lanterns and torches, its outspread branches cast dancing shadows across the law. The colonel was surrounded by an admiring crowd of officers and civilians—mostly older men. They were all more than certain of a swift Southern victory.

"I tell you, gentlemen, that the Yankee does not fight like the Southern man," Devere said. "He hardly fights at all. Why, not two days ago we ran off a pack of Yankees who had come down into our state. If we need only face more of the same, it will be a short war."

"Here, here!" said one of the gentlemen, raising his punch glass in salute.

"The key will be a swift and decisive battle," Devere said. "We must have one soon, to show that the Yankees have no stomach for war."

"When will we have battle, sir?"

"Before summer is over," Devere said, in a tone that indicated he knew more than he could reveal. "I am sure of it."

Flynn had heard enough. Thinking that he might join young Jay at the punch bowl, he turned away and found his path blocked by a plain woman who appeared to be hanging on Colonel Devere's every word.

She was well dressed, but in a less stylish manner than the other women.

"Excuse me, ma'am," Flynn said, attempting a bow. Wasn't that what he was supposed to do?

"Move," the woman said impatiently, and pushed past him to get closer to Devere. She seemed to be the only woman in the press of admirers. To Flynn's astonishment, she asked Devere a question.

"Colonel Devere, where do you think this battle will be?"

"Miss Carroll, isn't it? I can assure you that we will take the battle to the Yankees if need be."

"I have heard that General Johnston is in the Shenandoah Valley, marching north. Do you think that is where the battle will be? I hear that General Beauregard is building earthworks near Manassas Junction. Is there any truth to that?"

"You already seemed remarkably well informed, Miss Carroll." Devere laughed. "Why, if I didn't know better, I'd think that you were trying to gather information."

"And who would know better than you, Colonel?"

Devere's lips tightened into a smile. He seemed pleased by the compliment, but he didn't take the bait. "What General Beauregard does is up to the general, Miss Carroll."

The woman seemed ready to ask more questions, but one of the men said, "I declare, this punch is so strong that the next mosquito that bites me won't be able to fly straight." The others laughed, and the conversation turned away from military strategy. With a sour look of disappointment on her face, Miss Carroll slipped away.

Flynn watched her move to the edge of the garden, where she stood alone, surveying the party as if deciding who to question next. He soon followed and stood nearby, sipping from his glass of punch.

"You are playing a dangerous game, Miss Carroll," Flynn said quietly.

She had apparently been lost in her thoughts and looked up, startled. In the party lights, her eyes sparkled with both intelligence and impatience. "Who are you and what do you want?"

He got the impression that Miss Carroll was nothing, if not direct.

"Thomas Flynn. Lieutenant Flynn." He added for good measure, "At your service."

"That's a poor excuse for a uniform, Mr. Flynn." She raised her eyebrows. "Is that insignia *painted* on?"

He held up a sleeve of the preacher's former coat and shrugged. "Beggars can't be choosers, Miss Carroll."

"You sound Irish."

Flynn frowned. He knew that tone all too well. Also, he was a little annoyed that she had detected the accent that he worked hard to suppress at times like this. "I like to think of myself as American, by way of Ireland."

"You did not fully answer my question, Lieutenant Flynn. What do you want of me?"

"We have a mutual friend in Washington City who very much wishes you to return there."

"What mutual friend?"

Flynn hesitated.

"Well?"

"Rose Greenhow."

"Hah! You do know that the only reason she wants me back in Washington City is that she fears I am gathering information that will harm her precious Confederacy!"

Flynn looked around to make certain that no one had overheard. He said quietly, "In any case, I have been asked to accompany you back."

"Asked?"

"Paid."

"That makes you sound very much like a mercenary. Besides, how could you return to Washington? Aren't you supposed to be a Confederate officer?"

"I am what I must be, Miss Carroll. Circumstances change in these times."

"You are an interesting man, Lieutenant Flynn," she said. "I will take your offer to escort me back to Washington City under consideration—when the time comes."

"I would not wait too long, Miss Carroll."

She gave him a final look before drifting back toward the group surrounding Colonel Devere, who was holding forth on his opinions regarding the superiority of Confederate military tactics. From the sounds of it, a southern victory was a foregone conclusion. Standing at the edge of the crowd, Miss Carroll appeared to be soaking up every word.

Flynn shook his head. Miss Carroll was quite unlike any woman he had met before. She was clearly headstrong and intelligent—and yet, curiously oblivious to the danger that she was putting herself in.

He moved back toward the punchbowl. Jay had not moved from his position there. He was reeling a bit, laughing with a group of younger officers. The lot of them sounded drunk on the bourbon punch. Flynn overhead Jay saying, "I could hear one of those bullets pass so close that it cracked the air."

Before Flynn got there, Captain Blaine appeared, looking to refill his cup.

"Move aside, Warfield," he growled at Jay. "I'm sure everyone has tired of hearing about your so-called exploits the other day."

"Yes, sir." Jay turned to the other young men and said with a drunken grin, "That's Captain Blaine for you, boys, late to the battle-field, and late to the punchbowl!"

Jay's response brought howls of laughter from the other young officers.

Blaine turned, red-faced. He shook with anger, punch spilling from his cup. It did not help that Jay's comments had been made within earshot of Colonel Devere. The colonel turned his attention toward the scene unfolding around the punchbowl. Jay's words were more than an ill-considered comment. He had just called into question Captain Blaine's very standing in the legion.

For a Virginian like Blaine, reputation was everything.

"I will not be insulted," Blaine said.

"I'm sorry, sir. I—"

Blaine's eyes narrowed. "You need to learn to watch what you say, Warfield. I demand satisfaction."

The laughter died away. The smile faded on Jay's face and he looked momentarily sobered. By his mention of satisfaction, Blaine was invoking the code duello. Although dueling had fallen out of fashion above the Mason-Dixon Line, these Virginians still believed in settling their differences with a sword or a pistol.

Jay's apology wasn't enough for Blaine. He was clearly too embarrassed. Instead, he was challenging Jay to a duel.

Jay opened his mouth once, then twice, as if to respond, but no words came out.

Flynn stepped forward. "Come now, captain. This young fool here is deep in his cups. Let him apologize and that will be an end to it."

"He should learn to hold his tongue and his liquor. He has insulted me."

Flynn sighed. Blaine wasn't backing down. Flynn had no choice but to intercede on Jay's behalf by delivering an even worse insult. "The lad was just saying what everyone is already thinking, captain. You *were* late to the battle, after all."

"I was delayed," he said.

"Were you? Or were you late on purpose?"

"Are you calling me a coward?"

"If the boot fits, Captain, then put it on."

If it was possible, Blaine's face turned an even deeper shade of red. "I will see you at dawn tomorrow, sir."

Flynn nodded. "Aye, so you will."

Blaine turned and stormed out, jostling several people on his way toward the stables. He could soon be heard shouting for his horse.

Flynn ignored the stares he was getting and approached the young officers gathered around the punchbowl. He did notice Colonel Devere giving him a look that was hard to fathom. He either disapproved of the fact that two of his officers were fighting a duel—or he was worried. One of the civilians near Devere asked him a question, and his attention was diverted.

"I think you've had enough to drink, lad," Flynn said, relieving Jay of his cup of punch. "If you're to be my second tomorrow morning, I'll need you halfway sober."

He took Jay by the elbow and started to lead him away. It was time to retrieve their horses and ride back to camp. But before he could make good on their escape, he found Miss Carroll waiting for him.

"Go see to the horses, lad," Flynn ordered, giving Jay a gentle push in the direction of the stables. He turned to Miss Carroll. "Have you changed your mind about my offer to accompany you back to Washington City?"

"Not yet. Are you sure that you will even be available, depending on the outcome of your affair of honor tomorrow morning? I witnessed your exchange with Captain Blaine just now. Dueling, Lieutenant Flynn? That is unexpected, and perhaps not very wise."

"He would have killed that boy."

"I'm sure he would have," she agreed. "But now who is playing the dangerous game?"

"Not dangerous for me," he said with a grin. "It's Captain Blaine who should be worried."

"Don't be so sure of yourself," she snapped. She certainly had a very direct way of speaking. "The captain looks quite capable. Besides, if you kill his right-hand man, Colonel Devere is not going to be happy with you. You have a dilemma on your hands, Lieutenant Flynn."

"I'll keep that in mind."

"I'm sure that you'll figure something out. Meanwhile, do try not to get yourself shot. I'm beginning to like you, even if you are a mercenary," she said, lightly touching his arm before disappearing into the crowd of party-goers.

Flynn shook his head and watched her go, considering himself warned. The woman was right, he admitted.

Under the code duello, he had no choice but to fight Captain Blaine in the morning. If he chose not to fight, he would be labeled a coward. If he killed Blaine, there would be trouble. Then again, he certainly didn't want Blaine to kill *him*.

Miss Carroll had summed up the situation well. It was indeed a dilemma.

CHAPTER TWELVE

As if to make life seem all the more fleeting and bittersweet in the face of a duel, the July dawn was beguiling on Chimborazo Heights on the edge of Richmond. Morning mist still clung to the tall, dewy grass. Birds twittered in the trees or their gray shapes swooped low across the field, looking for a worm. Flynn envied the way that these simple creatures went about their business, oblivious to the cares of men.

The burning red ball of the rising sun slowly crested the treetops and rooflines of Richmond. In the distance, Flynn spotted the Confederate battle flag already flying from the capitol dome. The leadership of the new nation must be getting an early start, if they had even slept at all. He inhaled a deep breath and took in all the sights and sounds of the morning. It was indeed a rebel dawn, if he ever had seen one.

"You don't have to do this," Jay said.

"Of course I do, lad. What other choice is there?"

"I could apologize."

"What good would that do? It's not you that he's fighting the duel with, now is it?"

"*You* could apologize."

"But I'm not going to. Besides, I don't think Captain Blaine would settle for an apology. It's blood that he wants."

Jay didn't have a response to that. The lad was fighting a duel of his own this morning against a colossal hangover, brought on by the sweet punch that he had imbibed all too easily the night before. At the moment, the lad's hangover was winning. He looked sick. His boyish, normally handsome face was layered in shades of pale green. Jay took several steps away from Flynn, bent over, and vomited into the grass.

Flynn caught a whiff of stale bourbon. His stomach clenched and he was glad that he'd had nothing more this morning than strong black coffee.

"I'm such a fool," Jay groaned, swiping at his mouth with the back of his hand. "I drank too much, and I angered Captain Blaine in the first place by suggesting that he was late for that battle with the Union cavalry."

Flynn clapped him on the back. "*In vino veritas.*"

"There is truth in wine, all right. Especially if the wine is actually bourbon." Jay looked even greener when he mentioned the bourbon. He thought a moment, then added, "Because he is mortal and made of mould/He omits what he ought, and doth more than he should."

"Shakespeare again, I take it. Listen, Jay, your only mistake last night was calling that business the other day a battle. That was a skirmish we fought, and a small one at that."

"It seemed like a battle to me."

"If you ever witness a battle, lad, you'll soon understand the difference."

Jay straightened up. "Where the devil is he?"

"He'll be here. Don't you worry about that."

Briefly, Flynn had hoped that Colonel Devere might intervene and ordered them not to fight the duel. As the commanding officer, he certainly had good grounds for that. The possibility of losing two officers, dead or wounded, in a duel, just when they might soon be needed to fight the Union, should have been cause enough to cancel the duel. However, Devere was just the sort to believe in the necessity of defending one's honor with pistols or swords. For a Southerner like

Devere, the honor of his officers came first. The loss to the legion would be secondary.

Also, it nagged at Flynn that perhaps Devere had every confidence that Captain Blaine would emerge as the victor. If it came down to a fistfight, Flynn would undoubtedly win. He could pummel an ox into oblivion if need be. But duels were not fought with fists. They were fought with skill, usually with a pistol. Blaine had a reputation as a crack shot. Flynn was less skilled, which was why he liked the LeMat revolver with its lower barrel that delivered a shotgun blast. Of course, he wouldn't be fighting the duel with that gun, but with the dueling pistols supplied by Blaine.

Although Flynn had affected nonchalance with Jay, the truth was that he had slept fitfully. He wasn't afraid of fighting the duel and being killed—at least, not entirely. He supposed that he had a fifty-fifty chance of surviving. But there was nothing quite like an impending duel to prompt self-reflection. If he lived to see sunset, would he be the same man?

Flynn questioned the fact, once again, that he had allowed himself to be forced into uniform for a cause that he didn't believe in. He had already fought against Union troops. How many more times would he be called to do that?

Also, there was the matter of Anna Ella Carroll. He had finally met the woman last night and he had been intrigued. Miss Carroll was obviously intelligent, with a clear grasp of military strategy. However, her skills as a spy left something to be desired. She was much too obvious in how she gathered information. For now, she relied on men like Devere to dismiss her as an overly curious woman. But how long would that last? If she was truly found out to be a spy, her femininity would not protect her.

She also seemed stubborn, telling Flynn that she would return to Washington City in her own good time, despite his warnings and his offer to accompany her. Whether or not Rose Greenhow's motivations were to be trusted was another matter altogether. Maybe Mrs. Greenhow didn't wish for Miss Carroll to do any harm to the Confederate cause with her spying? None of that mattered to Flynn. He was being paid to bring Miss Carroll back home to safety. He would make every effort to earn his payment, short of kidnapping.

In the wee hours of the morning, Flynn's thoughts had turned outward. He had been raised Catholic, and had even received some education thanks to a benevolent priest who took a guilty pleasure in Shakespeare. His current lifestyle did not leave much room for religion, but he still knew the prayers by heart. He said them silently, mouthing the words until the sky began to turn gray and it was time to fight his duel.

* * *

THE DUELING GROUNDS on Chimborazo Heights were located west of East Franklin Street. Only a smattering of dwellings stood nearby because the bulk of the city itself lay in the other direction. The heights sloped down toward the James River, not far from the Tredegar Ironworks. Even at this early hour, a glow from the foundries hung over the hollow on the riverbank, and they could hear workmen in the factory, busy buildings guns for the Confederacy. The men down there worked nearly around the clock. Flynn had seen some of the vast factories in the northern states and knew that the sprawling Richmond ironworks would struggle to keep up.

A few farmers came past with their carts, getting an early start bringing their produce to market. The carts that went past were piled high with watermelons, sweet corn, and even peaches that were just coming into season. Some of the carts were driven by black men. Were they slaves or free? It was hard to know. Flynn suspected that any black man in Virginia was never truly free. In any case, the cart drivers eyed them with curiosity, but did not interfere with the two Confederate officers—one of whom was quite large and wearing a tattered coat that gave him a somewhat disreputable air.

The drivers had probably guessed their intentions, considering that this was a well-known dueling ground. Just two weeks before, Richmond had been abuzz about a notorious duel that had taken place here between young men who had once been friends. They had fallen out over the affections of a young woman. When the spurned young man wrote an off-color poem about the girl, it had brought on an affair of honor. The result was that one friend had been shot in the stomach and died an agonizing death two days later. The novice poet had been wounded in the hip. He lived, but found himself ostracized from polite society.

Jay interrupted Flynn's thoughts. "He's not coming."

"Patience, lad. He'll be here, all right. If he had as much punch as you, he may be feeling a little worse for wear this morning, is all."

Finally, they heard hoofbeats thundering up the road. Flynn saw Captain Blaine riding at a gallop, accompanied by three other men. It was just like Captain Blaine to make his arrival with fanfare. The only thing missing, Flynn mused, were trumpets.

Blaine reined in his horse and swung easily from the saddle. The other men with him were Sergeant Creighton, Lieutenant Tyler, and the legion's surgeon. The surgeon carried a medical bag.

"Top of the morning to you," Flynn said cheerfully. In truth, his greeting sounded a lot more cheerful than he felt. "I was just beginning to wonder if you had forgotten our appointment this morning."

"Small chance of that," Blaine said. His face looked grim. "Sergeant Creighton will be my second. I've also brought along Doctor Miller, to attend to any wounds."

Flynn nodded at Lieutenant Tyler. He was a studious and bespectacled young man who served as Colonel Devere's adjutant. "It looks as if you've also brought along a third."

"Lieutenant Tyler is here as an impartial observer, at Colonel Devere's insistence."

Lieutenant Tyler nodded uneasily at Flynn, looking as if he would rather be anywhere else. Flynn realized that Tyler had been sent to report back to Devere that the duelists had followed the rules of the Code Duello. The question was, which man did Devere doubt would follow the rules—Blaine, Flynn, or both?

Flynn winked at Devere's adjutant. "When the lead starts to fly, Lieutenant, just make sure to keep out of the way and you'll be all right."

The young lieutenant gulped.

Before the duel could get underway, they were interrupted by the arrival of a carriage.

"Who the devil is that?" Blaine asked.

The door to the carriage opened and to their astonishment, a woman stepped down. It was Miss Carroll.

It was hard to say which of the men was more surprised, but Flynn reacted first. He took off his hat and said, "Good morning, ma'am."

"This is no place for a woman!" Blaine shouted, clearly furious. "You must leave immediately."

"I will do no such thing," Miss Carroll said, standing her ground.

"This is foolishness!"

"The only foolishness I see is two men about to shoot at one another. If you insist on going through with this, then I insist on watching."

Now Blaine turned his anger on Flynn. "Did you invite her?" he hissed.

"No, I did not. For once, I'll agree with you that it's not a good idea. But from my limited acquaintance of Miss Carroll, she seems to be a woman of independent mind."

Blaine turned back to Miss Carroll. She had opened a parasol against the morning sun and did not seem inclined to be going anywhere. "Very well. Suit yourself. But don't blame me if you faint away from the sight of blood. Creighton, present the pistols."

Creighton stepped forward, holding an elegant walnut box. He opened it to reveal two old-fashioned pistols, cradled within the velvet-lined case. The pistols were beautifully made and appeared to be trimmed in silver. It would be just like the colonel to own a matched set of dueling pistols. It was hard to fathom how much such weapons had cost. Well, Flynn thought, at least we're going to kill each other in style.

"These are Colonel Devere's pistols," Tyler stammered. "He loaded them himself."

"How thoughtful of the colonel."

"The rules state that you can discharge the pistol and have your second reload it, if you prefer."

"I'm sure that the colonel knows what he's about."

Miss Carroll spoke up. "Do you think that's a good idea, Mr. Flynn? If I were you, I'd load my own pistol."

"Keep out of this!" Blaine shouted.

"Foolishness," she muttered.

"Would the seconds care to inspect the weapons?"

Sergeant Creighton stepped forward, took both of the pistols from the case and looked them over, and then nodded his approval.

"Warfield?"

"I'm sure they're fine," he said weakly.

"All right," Blaine said. "Go ahead and choose a pistol, Flynn."

Flynn reached for the case that Creighton held open before him. He hesitated. Did one pistol offer an advantage over the other? He chose the pistol closest to him in the box. It had a nice heft and balance. He was sure it would be a pleasure to shoot. Considering that Blaine was likely the superior marksman, that didn't bode well.

The rules of the duel were quickly agreed upon. The two seconds walked into the field and paced out two points that were fifty paces apart, taking care that the morning sun would not be in either man's eyes.

"With that dumb Irish ox out of the way, you'll be next," Sergeant Creighton whispered to Jay. "At the very least, I wouldn't count on being in the legion for much longer."

Jay gulped.

They marked the duelists' positions with flat stones. Flynn and Blaine would stand by the stones. Standing well to the side, Lieutenant Tyler would drop a handkerchief. The two men would then be free to fire at one another.

Blaine shed his coat, probably to give him better freedom of movement. His freshly laundered shirt gleamed a brilliant white in the morning sun. Blaine was slim from hours in the saddle. When he turned sideways, he made a poor target.

Flynn cast a look at Miss Carroll and decided to keep his coat on. His own shirt was patched and none too clean.

Resolutely, Flynn walked toward his stone. Maybe it was his imagination, but it seemed as if the birds had stopped singing. The sun was higher and he felt the heat of it on his face and neck. It promised to be a hot summer day. The question was, would he live to see it?

Having reached the stone, he turned sideways to present as small of a target as possible. Given his size, along with the bulky coat, that wasn't easy. He kept the pistol at his right side, waiting for the signal.

Across from him, Captain Blaine had taken up his position. He turned to present a narrow profile.

"Skinny bastard," Flynn muttered.

In the South, duels were often fought for show. The two duelists might only go through the motions to satisfy a question of honor. Killing one another was not their true intent.

But that was not the case here.

Flynn could see that Blaine's serious expression had been replaced by a cold smile. It was clear that the bastard fully intended to kill him.

Off to the side, Lieutenant Tyler raised the hand that held the handkerchief. Flynn watched for the signal from the corner of his eye, keeping his full attention on Captain Blaine. A single rivulet of sweat ran down the back of Flynn's neck. His senses were so elevated that it felt like a lava flow. Maybe he should have taken off the damn coat, after all.

The handkerchief fluttered down.

Instantly, Blaine raised the pistol and fired, faster than Flynn would have thought was possible. The sharp crack of the pistol shot broke the morning silence on Chimborazo Heights. The birds that had been busily greeting the new day launched themselves into the air, crying in alarm.

As if time had slowed, Flynn saw the stab of flame from Blaine's pistol. He heard the angry snap of the bullet.

Flynn felt the pistol ball pluck at his coat and thought, *I'm hit, dammit.* However, no pain registered. He looked down and saw a new hole in the coat, bigger than the collection of moth-holes. In his haste, Blaine had not taken time to aim carefully. His bullet had passed harmlessly through the fabric of the coat.

Flynn grinned. The look of smug satisfaction on Captain Blaine's face had given way to an expression of concern. He had fired his pistol and missed, while Flynn still held a loaded pistol. The Code Duello demanded that Blaine would have to stand still while Flynn took aim and returned fire.

Alarmed at what was about to take place, Tyler spoke up. "Gentlemen, please—"

"Quiet," Jay said.

Standing beside her carriage, even Miss Carroll had been left speechless. The driver watched with his mouth hanging open.

Bound by the rules of honor, there was nothing that the witnesses could do but watch.

Slowly and deliberately, Flynn leveled the pistol at Captain Blaine. He settled the silver bead on Blaine's chest. At this range, it was unlikely that he would miss. Blaine knew that, too. He closed his eyes, resigned to his fate.

Flynn squeezed the trigger. As he did so, he raised the pistol to a point well above Blaine's head. There was a sharp crack and the ball whistled harmlessly over the captain.

Blaine opened his eyes, apparently surprised to be alive.

"Captain Blaine, do you declare yourself satisfied?" Lieutenant Tyler asked.

The rules stated that because both men were unharmed, the offended party could ask that the pistols be reloaded and more shots taken until one of them was dead or wounded.

But Blaine appeared to have had enough. "I am satisfied."

It was only Sergeant Creighton who looked disappointed, scowling as he collected the pistols and returned them to their fancy case. Without another word, Captain Blaine and the sergeant mounted their horses and rode off, with Lieutenant Tyler hurrying to join them.

The three men were barely out of sight when Jay staggered away and vomited again.

"Are you all right, lad?"

"That was almost more than I could bear," Jay said. "When he fired so fast, I thought for sure that you were killed."

"Nothing that a needle and thread can't fix," Flynn said, poking a finger through the bullet hole and waggling it at Jay. "Then again, there are already so many holes in this coat that I'm not sure it's worth the trouble."

Miss Carroll approached. She seemed to have recovered her customary acerbic tone. "Well, don't expect me to mend your coat. I don't do that sort of thing."

"From our limited acquaintance, Miss Carroll, I didn't expect that you did much mending."

"You should have shot him. Duel or not, he'll be your enemy now."

"He was before."

"He'll be worse now."

"Maybe so," Flynn agreed. "But I couldn't shoot him down like a dog. Not like that. Not even someone like Blaine."

"I couldn't have, either," Miss Carroll agreed. "I think you did the right thing, although you didn't have to shoot so high over his head."

Flynn raised his eyebrows. It wasn't customary for women to observe a duel, let alone comment on dueling strategy.

"I'll keep that in mind for next time."

"In any case, I am glad you are not dead."

She returned to the carriage, climbed in, and gave a word to the driver, who set off for Richmond.

"Miss Carroll is certainly a most unusual woman," Flynn remarked.

Jay retched again.

CHAPTER THIRTEEN

As it turned out, Flynn saw Miss Carroll again sooner than he might have expected. This time, her carriage brought her to the headquarters of the Devere Legion. As soon as he realized who was getting out of the carriage, he walked over before Colonel Devere spotted her. The colonel would not be happy to see that she had turned up at his headquarters. Miss Carroll's questions at the party in Richmond had made him suspicious of her.

"Are you sure this is a good idea?" Flynn asked. Generally speaking, the only women who visited the legion's encampment were the wives and mothers of the cavalrymen. The officers who kept mistresses had to go into Richmond to see them. It was hard to know what she expected to gain from her impromptu visit. "You certainly attract a lot of attention to yourself for a spy."

"Sometimes the best way to hide is within plain sight."

From the porch of the farmhouse serving as the legion's headquarters, they heard a muttered curse and looked up to see Colonel Devere glaring at them. Just as Flynn had feared, her arrival was almost too much for Devere, who did not greet her with his usual courtesy. He greeted her curtly. "Why, Miss Carroll. This is quite unusual. What can I do for you?"

"I've come to see Lieutenant Flynn, now that he has survived that foolish business of the duel. But tell me, how long will it be until your legion rides out to fight the Yankees? Are you planning to ride north with General Beauregard?"

"Miss Carroll, these are matters that do not concern you," Devere said, scowling.

"If you say so, Colonel. Now, if you don't mind, I should like to visit with Lieutenant Flynn. He was regaling me the other night with the most interesting stories of his time in Italy. It seems that he is a real soldier, unlike some others."

Devere reddened and returned inside without saying another word.

"Devere has his doubts about you," Flynn said quietly, once they were alone. "He said so at the party in Richmond and you aren't helping by asking more questions today. If he can prove that you're a spy, he won't hesitate to hang a woman from that oak tree over there in the yard."

"Walk with me, Lieutenant Flynn."

They strolled the grounds of the farm property that served as the legion's headquarters. Miss Carroll did not take his arm when he offered it. "Do I look elderly or empty-headed to you, Lieutenant Flynn? I can quite manage walking on my own."

"I'm sure you can."

Flynn took no offense, but smiled to himself. He certainly hadn't entertained any question of romantic interest, but was only being courteous. Anna Ella Carrol was a plain, odd woman—perhaps too smart and direct for her own good. In the old days, she might have been accused of being the village witch whenever the milk curdled or the crops failed. At the moment, she seemed busy observing the number of horses and the training maneuvers taking place.

"You don't stop, do you?"

"I believe in the Union cause. Every bit of information may help. Are those carbines that I see? How many are there?"

"Not many. But never mind that. Miss Carroll, you need to stop this nonsense of playing at being a spy."

"Who said that I was playing? In any case, now that I have gathered a fair amount of intelligence, I need to get it into the right hands in Washington. I would like you to carry a dispatch for me back to Washington City."

"You mean to make me a spy as well," he said. He shook his head. "I won't be your errand boy, Miss Carroll. What I *will* do is escort you back to Washington, which is what I was asked to do in the first place."

"Paid to do, you mean. By none other than Rose Greenhow."

"That's true."

"Rest assured that I don't need anyone to escort me anywhere," she said. "Besides, I am not ready. There is a battle being planned and I must learn more."

"You don't need to be a spy to know that there's a big fight coming."

"I have information about it that will help the Union, or I hope that it will. If you won't carry a dispatch for me, then I shall have to find someone else."

"Like I said, you are playing a dangerous game."

"Considering that we are at war, there is no other kind of game."

They took a turn through the orchard, well within sight of a cavalry squad putting their horses through their paces. Some of the green apples had already fallen. The sickly sweet smell of rotting fruit had attracted yellow jackets that buzzed in their faces. They talked no more of dispatches or spying. Instead, she asked about his experiences in Italy. Flynn asked what it had been like to be the daughter of a governor.

Miss Carroll gave a rare smile. "My father was the perfect scholar. He was quite happy with his books or debating the fine points of legislation in the statehouse. He was not a good politician. I think he was elected mainly because he wouldn't cause trouble for anyone. He was even worse as a businessman."

They had returned to her carriage. Flynn asked, "What are you good at, Miss Carroll?"

"I am still finding out," she said. She fell quiet and gave him an appraising look. "You know, I have been critical of the Irish in the past, considering that they are all papists and drunkards. Perhaps I could make an exception in your case."

"Just let me know when you are ready to go back to Washington."
She nodded, then rolled away once more toward Richmond.

* * *

THE VISIT from Miss Carroll soon caused problems for Flynn when he found himself summoned to Devere's headquarters. The colonel sat behind his desk, glaring at Flynn, who was forced to remain standing. Tyler stood to one side, once again serving as a witness.

"Lieutenant Flynn, you are taxing my patience," Colonel Devere said.

"Sir?"

"When you provoked Captain Blaine to a duel, I looked the other way. Matters of honor must be settled appropriately. But do not think that you will duel your way to a promotion in this legion."

"I think nothing of the sort, sir."

"Lieutenant Tyler observed the duel on Chimborazo Heights," Devere said, glancing at his adjutant. "He reported that it was settled to everyone's satisfaction. While I appreciate your restraint in aiming your shot above Blaine's head, you will not fight another duel against one of my officers. My officers are needed to fight Yankees. Are you in agreement, Lieutenant Flynn?"

"Yes, sir."

"But it is not only the duel that concerns me. I won't have that Carroll woman snooping about the camp. Simply put, I do not trust her."

"Colonel, I can assure you that her coming here was not my idea."

"Tyler says that she also came to see the duel."

"She is a woman who sets her own course, sir."

"What is your interest in this woman, Flynn? She certainly seems to have taken an interest in *you*."

Flynn realized that he was on dangerous ground. Devere was already suspicious of the woman, although he had not come out and called her a spy. Flynn had no desire to be painted with the same brush.

"I've heard that she is a woman of some means," Flynn said slowly.

"Ha!" Devere seemed amused, evidently buying Flynn's romantic interest at face value. "She's virtually a pauper. She comes from an old and distinguished family—I'll grant you that. But if I were you, I would look elsewhere for a rich dowry. Besides, I wouldn't have thought she was your sort."

"Who would be my sort?" Flynn wondered, genuinely curious.

Devere didn't answer, but simply shook his head. "In any case, we have other matters to attend to. In two days, we ride out to join the attack on Washington City."

"It's about time, sir."

"Indeed it is," Devere said. "Whatever you do, don't go giving that information to Miss Carroll. You see, I believe that she is a spy for the Union."

There it was, Flynn thought. "A spy, sir? Are you sure?"

"I have my suspicions. Look at all the questions she asks. Her purpose goes beyond idle curiosity."

"What will you do, sir?"

"Do? That should be obvious, Flynn. If that woman is a spy she will be hanged."

* * *

ALTHOUGH THE LEGION was already busy with preparations for the advance, all of the officers and many of the men were given passes to visit Richmond. This had been the opportunity that Flynn had been waiting for to see that young Warfield did not ride into battle without being properly bedded.

Also, he hoped that he could warn Miss Carroll that Devere suspected her of spying. All that Devere needed was proof. Flynn would try to encourage her again to leave Richmond. The sooner, the better. As far as he could see, she was walking a tightrope. One false step would spell disaster.

But he would need to be careful what he told her. Flynn could see the trap that Devere had set. If Miss Carroll made it known that she was aware that the legion would ride out, it would be plain that the information had come from Flynn.

The city bustled with activity and excitement. Although Devere had sworn Flynn to secrecy about the plans to move on Washington, Flynn wondered how much of a secret it was that the Confederate army was finally marching to war. There seemed to be an air of abandon in the streets. It was the devil-may-care attitude of soldiers about to test themselves in battle. Others seemed to act as if the war had already been fought and won. Certainly, the saloons and whorehouses were filled to overflowing.

"What are we doing here?" Jay asked.

"You'll find out soon enough, lad. But first, I must pay a visit to Miss Carroll."

Jay rolled his eyes. "Why her?"

"It won't take long."

She had given him a calling card with her address on it. He was surprised to see that it was just a modest boarding house for women. Maybe Devere was right and Anna Ella Carroll, daughter of one of Maryland's most celebrated families, was little more than a pauper.

As it turned out, the raucous mood of the city had reached here as well. A group of rough-looking soldiers came past, clearly drunk. Flynn gave them a wide berth.

A cart driver wasn't as lucky in avoiding them. The driver was an older black man, carefully minding his own business and staring straight ahead.

"You there!" A soldier shouted at the cart. "Where are you going in such a hurry? You damn near ran me over!"

The group of soldiers quickly circled the cart, one of them taking the horse by the bridle. The cart driver desperately looked around, but there was no help for him here.

Flynn sighed. He was almost at Miss Carroll's door.

"Wait here, lad," he ordered Jay, then turned back.

He could see that the drunken soldiers were preparing to drag the cart driver from his seat.

"Moses!" Flynn shouted. "There you are!"

The soldiers turned. In the dim light, they could see his officer's coat. They could also see his size.

The driver turned to stare at Flynn, wide-eyed with fright, but he managed to keep his wits about him.

"Yes, sir," said the driver, who had never laid eyes on Flynn before "Here I am."

One of the drunken soldiers turned in surprise. "Who the hell are you?"

"You're late," Flynn said, turning his attention back to the cart driver. "You need to get these supplies to the legion immediately! Now, be on your way before I lose my temper."

"Yes, sir."

The driver flicked the reins and drove off.

Flynn gave the soldiers his best officer's scowl. "Do you men have passes, or shall I call for the provost?"

Grumbling, the men began pawing through their pockets in search of the passes giving them permission to be on the streets. Flynn gave their papers a cursory glance, then waved them off. "Go on then! Drink up while you can."

Returning to Miss Carroll's doorstep, Jay was watching, one hand gripping the pistol in his holster. "I thought I might be needing this. What did you care about a cart driver?"

"We're all cart drivers at one time or another, lad."

Before they could knock, Miss Carroll came out on the porch. "I heard the commotion in the street," she said. "To my great surprise, there was Lieutenant Flynn, chasing off some drunken soldiers to save a cart driver. What a curious man you are, Mr. Flynn. What brings you to my doorstep?"

"Another warning," he said, lowering his voice. "You need to leave Richmond, the sooner, the better."

"I have arranged for a courier to carry some of my messages to Washington so that I can stay longer. As I said before, I shall leave when I am ready and not a moment before."

"Don't be foolish."

"Says the man who just risked life and limb saving a cart driver. Good evening, Lieutenant Flynn."

The door closed, leaving Flynn standing on the doorstep with his hat in his hand.

"What was that all about?" Jay wanted to know.

"Pigheadedness, that's what." Flynn sighed. "With any luck, that's the last we'll see of that woman. We're riding out in two days' time. But first, we've other business to attend to."

* * *

RICHMOND'S BROTHELS and whorehouses were thriving now that the city was flooded with soldiers. Flynn returned to one that he had visited before, run by a woman named Maude. Like Flynn, she was Irish, and had become quite the independent businesswoman. Big-boned, at least six feet tall, and closer to fifty than to forty, she still managed to cut a striking figure as she greeted them at the door of her house on East Franklin Street. As far as Flynn knew, she owned the substantial brick house and all its furnishing outright—quite a long way from the crumbling stone cottage in Connemara that she had fled as a young woman during the height of the famine.

"Hello, Tom," she said. "Nice to see you again. Who's your friend?"

"This is Jay. It's his first time," he added with a wink.

"Oh, I'll be sure to take good care of him."

They followed her into a well-appointed parlor, filled with new-looking brocade furniture. There were three girls there, all much younger than Maude. One of them sat on a sofa with a young officer. He scarcely paid Flynn and Jay any attention because his eyes were focused on the red-haired young woman who sat perched on the edge of the sofa in her bright-red undergarments. Jay's eyes widened at the sight.

"Hello girls," Flynn said.

They greeted him with some familiarity. A woman with carefully curled raven-black hair asked, "Where have you been? We haven't seen you for a while."

He stretched out his arms to make his uniform more obvious. "I've been playing at soldier, can't you see?"

Maude studied him critically. "Sure, and that has got to be the worst uniform that I've seen yet. It looks like you should have let the moths have the rest of it."

Flynn sighed. The coat had not been improved by the bullet hole that he'd gotten on Chimborazo Heights. "You may be right about that."

Maude turned business-like. "Cherie, see to our young friend here." The woman with the dark tresses smiled and reached for Jay's hand. If he blushed any redder, Flynn feared that the lad's face might burst into flame. She led him off away down a hallway.

Maude turned to Flynn. "What about you? I'm sure you didn't come here just for that lad's sake. Priscilla is free."

Flynn looked at the girl on the sofa, who gave him a shy smile. She was a little bony for his taste, however. He turned back to Maude with a grin. "Do you think Priscilla can mind the store for a while?"

"You heard the man, Priscilla. You're in charge," Maude said, smiling. She flung a big arm in the direction of her own boudoir. "Don't worry, this won't take long."

Flynn laughed. "Och, don't be so harsh. Besides, I wouldn't be so sure about that."

Maude laughed. "You always were full of yourself, Tom Flynn. Just leave that damn coat in the parlor. I don't want the moths eating my carpets."

CHAPTER FOURTEEN

TWO DAYS AFTER RETURNING FROM RICHMOND, FLYNN AWOKE TO what he thought was the rumble of artillery in the distance. For a moment, he had dreamt that he was back at the Battle of Castelfidardo, hearing the enemy guns pummel the troops of Pope Pius IX. They had been badly outnumbered, but the Irish troops fought like lions. Before the day was over, hundreds on both sides lay dead or wounded. He jerked awake at the sound, then realized it was only thunder.

"What is it?" asked Jay, who had been sleeping nearby.

"Thunder, that's what. Sounds like we get to ride in the rain," Flynn said.

The day had arrived for Devere's Legion to ride out and join the war. The Union army under General McDowell had marched into Virginia in the first major maneuver of the war. That threat needed to be met and every Confederate soldier was needed, considering that the Union forces outnumbered them so far.

Reveille had not been sounded, but Flynn began to roll up his blanket. There was no point in trying to get back to sleep.

The sounds of thunder faded when the morning storm kept to the west. Not so much as a drop of rain fell. When the sun emerged, it turned the overcast sky steamy. Thick dew covered the grass. Already, insects sang in the heat.

Typical Virginia summer weather. It promised to be a long, hot, dusty day in the saddle.

"Make sure you fill your canteen," Flynn said, then thrust his canteen at Jay. "Might as well fill mine while you're at it. We're going to need them today."

Around them, other men were now awake and like Jay, lining up to fill their canteens from the well in the yard. The legion soon gathered in a field near the farmhouse. It seemed like a simple matter to gather a company of cavalry and set them on the road, but there were more than men and horses to consider. There were also provisions to feed the legion, and even wagons filled with forage for the horses. The men grew bored and hot in the morning sun, while the horses grazed where they could.

Devere rode about impatiently, barking orders. Captain Blaine rode to and fro, too busy to make his usual glares in Flynn's direction. Since the duel, Blaine had kept his distance, but the looks he gave Flynn made it clear that there was unfinished business between them. Instead of being grateful that Flynn had fired over his head and deliberately missed him, the captain seemed to be plotting some measure of revenge.

Maybe Miss Carroll had been correct when she'd said that Flynn should have shot the man when he'd had the chance.

But Blaine had no time to nurse his grudges this morning. He was finally able to get the company's baggage train organized, more or less, and the legion finally rode out.

They were not alone. Carriages had arrived from Richmond, filled with well-wishers and even relatives of the cavalry troops. Some cheered and waved small flags.

Blaine gave the civilians a show, drawing his sword and proclaiming, "We ride to Washington or the devil!"

This drew more cheers from the cavalry. Even Jay let out a whoop.

"You're one of the last people I thought would cheer Captain Blaine," Flynn muttered.

"My father used to say that even a broken clock is right twice a day."

Flynn had to admit that Blaine certainly looked the part, riding near the head of the column in his tailored uniform with the hand-stitched gold braid, his shiny riding boots, and of course, a new plume in his hat. Even Blaine's horse, a beautiful chestnut mare, seemed to hold her head high. There was no doubt that Devere's Legion would be victorious in the coming battle.

The fanfare did not last for long as the summer heat increased. Soon, the cavalrymen slouched in their saddles, or took off their sharp-looking hats to mop their brows. Even the countryside seemed tired of them. Although crowds had come out from Richmond to see them off, the country people had made themselves scarce at the approach of Devere's Legion. The farms they passed had a deserted look. Country people were naturally suspicious of strangers passing by. Flynn suspected that chickens had been locked into henhouses, horses had been hidden in the woods, and possibly even daughters had been tucked away out of sight.

The only people who ran to greet them beside the road were small boys who didn't know any better. Some of them would live well into the next century and regale their grandchildren with stories of how they once had seen the Confederate cavalry riding out in all its glory.

"I wonder if my brother is riding with McDowell?" Jay wondered. "I certainly hope so."

Flynn shook his head. "Are you still that eager to fight your brother?"

"I want to prove to Sid for once and for all who the better man is."

"It won't get your girl back."

"That's not the point."

"Besides, I would hope by now that you realize there's more than one woman in the world. Our field trip in Richmond should have taken some of the mystery out of women."

Jay blushed. "That doesn't mean I still don't have something to prove to Sid."

"Someday you'll realize that the only man you have to prove anything to is yourself."

"You really are full of blarney, Flynn."

"I can tell you another thing, lad. If he's half the rider you are, we're in for a nasty fight."

"If you say so. I just hope McDowell's troops don't all start running before we get there."

"We should be so lucky," Flynn said. "Do you think you're going to a jousting tournament? Never mind the flags and banners, sonny, because in the end, battle is not a pretty thing. Battle is confusion and dirty tricks, screams and booming guns, the stink of gunpowder and fresh blood. Even the bravest man will cry for his mother as he falls wounded. The man who has turned his back on God will pray. I suppose we humans are naturally prone to anger and violence, it's in our nature as much as song and love, but once you've seen the wreckage of a battlefield, you'll realize that we ought to know better than to go about killing one another just because some king or president says we should."

Jay grinned and shook his head. "Don't let Captain Blaine hear you talk like that or he'll challenge you to another duel."

"Captain Blaine might just be one of the first to get a rude awakening."

They rode on in silence for another mile or two. Dust began to grit between Flynn's teeth.

A few scouts had ridden out from the main column to explore the farms and make sure that Yankee cavalry wasn't waiting in ambush, although that seemed unlikely this deep into Virginia. Since the skirmish with the Union cavalry a few days ago, no one had reported seeing any blue-coated troops. It was clear that the Yankees must have withdrawn closer to the Potomac.

Toward noon, the monotony was broken when a shout came from a group of these scouts, riding hard for the main column. They led a horse on which a man was struggling to stay in the saddle because his hands were tied behind him.

"Colonel Devere! Sir! We have caught a spy!"

Devere called for the column to halt, then rode out to meet the scouts. Curious, several officers gathered around, Flynn among them. A spy? It seemed unlikely to Flynn. Probably some farmer who didn't want to give up the contents of his smokehouse, he thought.

Colonel Devere seemed to be of the same opinion. "You had better not be wasting my time, Corporal. I've halted the whole column for this nonsense."

But the scout seemed convinced. "He's a spy, sir. No doubt about it."

The man in question hadn't said a word. He did not look like a farmer, but had a softness about him like a shopkeeper. He wore a frock coat that had seen better days and had lost his hat somewhere, revealing a balding pate that was already beginning to turn red in the sun.

"Why do you say this man is a spy?"

"We found this on him, sir," said the excited trooper, thrusting a thick envelope at the colonel.

Devere moved his horse closer and took the envelope. The document within contained several handwritten pages. He read for a moment, his face growing darker with each page that he saw.

"Curse that woman!" he roared. "I knew she was not to be trusted."

Flynn was confused by the colonel's outburst. What woman? The accused spy that the scouts had caught was clearly a middle-aged man.

Devere hadn't been able to tear his eyes away from the documents. When he was finally finished, he handed the envelope to his adjutant, then turned his attention to the bound man on horseback. "You are a spy!"

"I am only a courier," the man replied in a quaking voice. "How was I to know what the envelope contained?"

"Lies and deceit!" Devere exclaimed. "That harpy asked you to carry this message!"

"Harpy, sir?"

"Why, Anna Ella Carroll. How do you know this woman?"

Flynn felt his heart sink at the mention of Miss Carroll's name. She had said something to him about relying on a courier. Had she been foolish enough to put her name on the documents?

The prisoner said, "We have mutual friends in Richmond. When she heard that I was riding to Washington, she came to me and asked me to carry this letter for her. I had no idea of the contents, I can assure you."

"Yet you admit you were going to Washington," Devere said pointedly. "Why?"

The prisoner took his time answering. His eyes had the look of a man trying to find his way across a stream by jumping from one slippery rock to another. "I have business there."

"Business with the Yankees, you mean! To whom were you supposed to deliver this letter?"

"To President Lincoln, or short of that, his secretary."

"Lincoln!" Devere barked out a laugh. "You have high hopes, don't you?"

"Miss Carroll said he would be expecting it."

"Didn't it occur to you that this letter might have something to do with the war?"

This time, the prisoner didn't bother to deny it. His silence seemed to be an admission of guilt.

Colonel Devere appeared to have heard enough. He snorted in disgust.

"What do you want me to do with him, sir?" Captain Blaine asked the colonel.

"There's no doubt that this man is a spy," Devere replied. "The penalty for being a spy is clear."

Looking frightened now, the prisoner spoke up. "I'm not a spy! Like I said, she just told me it was a letter. If it's a spy you want, then you should be looking for Miss Carroll."

"Is she still in Richmond?"

"I believe that she is heading to Washington."

"Then why didn't she carry the letter herself?"

Again, the prisoner hesitated. "The letter I had was a copy. She said something about wanting to make sure that her correspondence got through in case she was delayed."

"Damn that woman! We'll be sure to hang her when we find her. For now, you will have to do. Lieutenant Tyler, take him to that tree over there."

"Wait a minute. Please! I beg you—"

"Have some dignity, sir," the adjutant said to the condemned man. "I'll say a prayer with you, if you want."

"What I want is for you to let me go! Please!"

But the prisoner's pleas fell on deaf ears. Normally, Devere might have made something of a spectacle of the hanging of a spy. In normal times, a good hanging was always an excuse for a public event. People would come from miles around, even bringing their children—the idea was that a hanging provided a good moral lesson. Even in Virginia, it was unusual for common criminals to be hanged, so those sentenced to the gallows were usually guilty of really heinous crimes, like murder, rape, and horse thieving. Food and lodging would be sold, giving local businesses a boost.

There was no time for any of that. There was a war on. Hanging a spy was simply a matter that needed to be seen to before the legion rode out.

The officers gathered around a tall, lonely oak that grew beside the dusty road. The scars on the trunk told the tale of how many lightning strikes the tree must have endured over the years.

A rope was found and thrown over a sturdy branch about ten feet above the ground. Hastily, a noose was tied into one end of the rope, then slipped over the neck of the condemned man, who was still in the saddle, bareheaded, his hands tied behind him. He had been busy with a stream of pleas for his life, but Sergeant Creighton tightened the knot against his Adam's apple and shut him up by making it hard for him to speak.

Some of the cavalrymen dismounted and gathered around, curious to see the hanging up close.

Devere presided over the preparations, watching it all with cold eyes and deaf to the prisoner's desperate begging, which now came out in a harsh croak. His glance fell on Flynn and the colonel said, "Lieutenant Flynn, come here a minute."

Flynn had dismounted to stretch his legs. Reluctantly, he approached the colonel.

"Sir?"

Devere bent ever so slightly in the saddle and said quietly, "Flynn, if I thought for a minute that you had anything to do with this business involving Miss Carroll, you'd be swinging right beside this fool. Is there anything that you want to tell me?"

Flynn could have told him a lot of things—how he had been enlisted by the Confederate spy Rose Greenhow to bring Miss Carroll back to Washington, or about the fact that he knew very well that the woman was spending her time in Richmond spying. He might have added that he thought Miss Carroll was arrogant, or possibly just naive.

What he said was, "No, Colonel. If we find Miss Carroll on the road to Washington, I'll help you hang her myself."

Devere nodded, seemingly satisfied. "With any luck, that's just what we'll do."

"Yes, sir."

The colonel turned his attention back to the proceedings. Beneath the prisoner, the horse felt the freedom of not having a hand on his reins and fidgeted, threatening to wander off and leave the prisoner suspended by his neck.

Devere glared at the prisoner. "Any last words?"

"Please, sir," the prisoner wheezed, straining against the knot that was tight against his throat. "Don't do this. I'm not—"

Devere cut him off, raising his voice to address the men. "Today we have caught a spy, carrying secrets to the north. He has admitted as much. A spy is the worst sort of traitor and can't be trusted by either side. Even an enemy soldier on the battlefield has honor, but not a spy. There's only one punishment for being a spy, which we are carrying out."

The colonel drew his revolver and fired a single shot into the air.

Beneath the prisoner, the horse startled and left him hanging from the rope. His feet weren't tied together, so he kicked frantically as if trying to reach the ground below. But his movements soon slowed and finally stopped. The body swung gently from side to side in the shade of the big oak.

The cavalrymen watched quietly. Some took off their hats out of pure habit as a sign of respect for the dead. Flynn noticed that Jay was one of them.

A few other men spat tobacco juice into the dust. They had no use for spies.

"What should we do with him, sir?" the adjutant asked quietly. "Should we cut him down?"

Colonel Devere shook his head. "Let the buzzards have at him. He can hang as a warning to others. This is what happens when Devere's Legion catches a spy. God willing, we'll hang that meddling Anna Ella Carroll next."

CHAPTER FIFTEEN

IN THE PAGES OF A LEDGER BOOK, THE UNION ARMY SEEMED TO have every advantage. At least sixty-one regiments of volunteers waited in Washington City, along with more than 1500 regulars. As a base of operations, Washington was in close proximity to what promised to be the first battlefield of the war, making for easy supply lines.

But in the end, the numbers and logistics were nothing but a paper tiger. Many of the troops were ninety-day enlistments whose term was coming to an end. They were less than eager for a fight and had already turned their thoughts to returning home. They'd had enough of soldiering. Some even marched in the opposite direction when their term of enlistment ran out on the appointed day of battle. President Lincoln was calling for longer terms of enlistment, but those fresh troops had not yet arrived in any meaningful way.

To make matters worse, the troops were often poorly trained and badly led. There wasn't a great deal of military training that could take place in three months, especially not when much of that time had been taken up with traveling from their home states to the capital. Many of the commanding officers were political appointees. At the company level, officers were often elected, making it difficult to impose any meaningful discipline. As a result, many soldiers did as they pleased, treating their time in Washington as a lark by drinking and visiting brothels when they should have been learning to be military men.

If the men were rowdy, welcoming the time away from their parents or wives, the officers might be worse. They did just as much drinking and whoring, but at more expensive bars and brothels. Some were busy lining their pockets by selling supplies and even food meant for their men, leaving the soldiers ill-equipped and hungry.

Observing the army for *The London Times*, the journalist William Howard Russell just shook his head. He had covered other wars, including the bitter Crimean War, and what he saw in the United States was far from an organized army. He wrote that he didn't know whether to be amused or aghast.

Even General McDowell despaired of how he was going to lead these troops to victory. He kept such thoughts to himself, but his close staff could see that the issue weighed heavily on him. Shorthanded, he found himself running errands of the sort that should have been handled by an aide. Just hours before the battle, when he should have been in Washington or even in Virginia, he was in Annapolis, trying to arrange railroad cars to carry reinforcements. He should have been focused on strategy for the upcoming battle, rather than basic logistics.

In part, he was hobbled by the popularity of General Winfield Scott. The tall and imposing general certainly looked the part of military hero. Many saw General Scott, the overall commanding general, as the military genius who would lead the Union to victory. All eyes seemed to be on the charismatic old general who had been nicknamed, "Old Fuss and Feathers." McDowell was seen only as an afterthought, or even worse, a lackey. He was such an unassuming figure that it wasn't unusual for the troops not to salute him—not out of disrespect, but simply because they scarcely noticed the one-star general.

For all of General Scott's considerable accomplishments, he was a man in his twilight years at seventy-four years of age. There was no getting around the fact that he was too old and fat to mount a horse. If he managed to lead troops in battle, it would have to be from a carriage rather than horseback.

His gout prevented him from walking much. Instead, he lay on a chaise in his office and busily pointed at the maps on the wall while a servant fanned him in the summer heat. He envisioned encircling the rebellious South and crushing it in a plan that some called "Scott's Great Snake." Otherwise, he made very little contribution to preparations for fighting the war or even helping his troops plan in any meaningful way for the approaching battle on Washington's doorstep.

One of those soldiers preparing for war was Lieutenant Sid Warfield, who had found himself enlisted in the First Delaware, a cavalry unit made up of recruits from Maryland and Delaware. Many of the volunteers from his home state had chosen to wear gray, rather than blue, but he had found a military home with the Delawareans.

"Do you think the boys are ready, sir?" he asked his captain. The two men were riding side by side through the regiment's encampment near Alexandria.

Captain Ott laughed. Like most of the officers, he was a volunteer rather than a professional. Before the war, he'd been a successful peach farmer on the Delmarva Peninsula. "They'll be ready enough, lieutenant. All we need is one good fight from them, anyhow. One battle should be enough to win the war and decide the matter for good."

"Tomorrow?"

Rumors had flown fast and furious, it was true, but it finally seemed that the troops were going to ride out.

"Get some rest," the captain said. "We'll ride out before dawn and provide screening against any enemy cavalry that tries to harass our flanks."

"Yes, sir."

The captain gave his young lieutenant a sidelong look. He knew that Sid's younger brother had run away to join the Confederate army. "Any word from that brother of yours?"

"Only a brief letter home to let our parents know that he was near Richmond."

"He's a soldier, then?"

"He joined the cavalry, sir. I believe it's a unit called Devere's Legion."

Captain Ott nodded thoughtfully, then sighed. "This war has been a terrible thing, turning brother against brother, and even father against son. Tell me, what made your brother into a rebel?"

"I'm afraid that it had less to do with politics and more to do with me."

"How do you figure that, son?"

Sid reddened slightly. "We both shared an affection for the same young lady."

"But you're engaged!"

"Yes."

"Ah," the captain said, nodding in understanding. "You mean you are engaged to the young lady in question. Your brother was the unlucky suitor."

"I'm afraid that Jay did not take it very well."

"Considering that he ran away and joined the Confederate cavalry, I would say you're right."

"My younger brother always was hot-headed."

"What if you have to face him tomorrow?"

"I've thought of it, sir." He added resolutely, "Rest assured that I will do my duty."

Sid rode on in silence, lost in his thoughts, wondering what the next day would bring. Like most soldiers, he hoped that he would be up to the task. But more than that, he was hoping against hope that he would not see his brother on the battlefield. After all, it was one thing to promise your commanding officer that you would do your duty, and quite another to imagine seeing your own brother in your pistol sights.

* * *

FOR THE CIVILIANS in the city, the next day promised only excitement. Hundreds were preparing to ride out and watch the battle that was sure to take place. Not a horse or carriage for hire was to be found by late afternoon and those who had managed to procure even the most swaybacked horse from one of the city's stables had paid dearly.

One of those planning to make the journey into Virginia was Congressman Alfred Ely of New York, who had paid twenty-five dollars for his carriage, a sum that made even a rich congressman raise his eyebrows. But he paid it, determined that he wouldn't miss the battle. He looked forward to seeing the rebellion brought to a quick end, the slaves freed once and for all, and the Union reunited.

The *London Times* correspondent noted, "The French cooks and hotel-keepers have arrived at the conclusion that they must treble the prices of their wines and of the hampers of provisions which the Washington people are ordering to comfort themselves at their bloody Derby." It was a cynical observation from a man who had witnessed war in Europe.

Like many others, Ely ordered sandwiches from his hotel and even a bottle of wine. It also went without saying that he already had a flask of whiskey in his pocket—no self-respecting congressman would be caught without that. The tall congressman wore a fashionable linen duster over his light summer suit. Overall, he cut a rather dashing figure with his masculine good looks, long salt-and-pepper hair, and neatly trimmed beard.

"No reason not to enjoy ourselves," he told another congressman who planned to accompany him. "We don't want to have to forage for our food."

"Then why are you bringing your shotgun?" his fellow congressman asked. "Do you plan on shooting some doves along the way?"

"We may encounter Confederate soldiers," Ely pointed out. "In case you haven't noticed, we are representatives of what they consider to be an enemy government. You know what Machiavelli said. 'Before all else, be armed.' "

"Shotguns and sandwiches," his fellow congressman grumped. "You'd think we *were* going dove hunting, rather than going to watch the war begin."

"My wife is not pleased that we are going to war on a Sunday," Ely said. "She claims no good will come of it."

"Tell that to the Southerners. You might as well ask it not to rain on the Lord's Day as put off the war."

Ely nodded; his friend had a point. But the simple truth of the matter was that his wife's words had made him uneasy. He couldn't help but agree that the Almighty would not be pleased about fighting on Sunday. He wondered what the consequences might be?

The two congressmen weren't the only ones preparing to witness the battle. Even whole families were planning picnics, without any thought given to the fact that war was a bloody business, rather than a spectator sport. Throughout Washington City, a kind of carnival excitement seemed to make the very air crackle.

Less than a day later, the scene would prove to be very different, indeed.

* * *

AT HER HOUSE on the corner of 16th and K streets, Mrs. Rose Greenhow was perhaps even busier than General McDowell. Her focus was on gathering information that might help General Beauregard. One after another, a steady stream of clerks, Union officers of various ranks, and officials of dubious loyalties visited her parlor. Some unwittingly let slip important information about everything from troop movements to the foibles of various officers.

There were even a few who tried to best the Southern spy at her own game by planting false information or gaining something useful from her. Not all battles were being fought with muskets and swords.

Her house was being watched and there were now even guards posted outside. The soldiers walked up and down the street, carrying rifles with fixed bayonets over their shoulders, On the one hand, the guards kept an eye on the comings and goings at the house. They also discouraged angry Northerners who'd had enough of a Southern spy in their midst. In the days leading up to the battle, her house had been nicknamed "Fort Greenhow." It was almost like an unofficial Confederate embassy in the heart of the Union capital city.

At the moment, she was entertaining a major who didn't seem to have any troops to command, or any real duties, but abundant time to spend in the drawing rooms of various known Southern sympathizers. She was sure that he was a creature of Allen Pinkerton, who was quickly becoming the North's spymaster.

"McDowell is sending ten thousand troops up the James River to take Richmond," the major declared. "If only General Beauregard knew, he could send half his force to meet them."

"How interesting," she replied, in a tone that indicated it wasn't interesting at all. She knew the major was only hoping that his false information would reach General Beauregard's ears, prompting him to weaken his position in Manassas by sending troops elsewhere. "More tea?"

Some of her visitors made no pretense about the fact that they were gathering information to help the Confederate forces. Just that morning, one of them had brought her a small map showing the plans for the movement of all McDowell's troops, along with unit strengths and where they would be positioned. As far as she could tell, it was quite a windfall.

She had folded the map into a tiny square, then wrapped it in a bit of black silk and sewed it up with her own hands so that it looked like a sachet. A young woman whom Rose knew to be another Southern sympathizer had then tucked the map into her hair and delivered it to Beauregard's headquarters, not more than 30 miles away from this parlor. The information might not win the battle, but it would not hurt.

This would be no random clash of arms. Mrs. Greenhow had a good grasp of military strategy. She saw that the Confederates had chosen their ground wisely, positioning themselves near the Orange and Alexandria Railroad. This provided them with access to transportation—both supplies and troops—from deeper in Virginia.

Already, the railroads had proved vital for moving supplies and men. It was the railroad that had brought troops to Baltimore on the day of that fateful Pratt Street riot. When that route had closed, trains carried reinforcements to Washington from Annapolis, where they had arrived by steamer on the Chesapeake Bay. Near that Southern railroad, Beauregard's men were now dug in along the banks of Bull Run and awaiting the Union troops.

On the sofa across from her, the mysterious major sipped his tea and eyed her watchfully, like a cat eyes a canary. She lowered her voice conspiratorially. "I have heard that two gunboats loaded with Confederate soldiers are going to come up the Chesapeake Bay and then the Potomac to make a direct attack on Alexandria while McDowell is otherwise engaged." She smiled pleasantly, pleased that she had fabricated that information on the spot. Southerners always had been good storytellers. "Such rumors that one hears!"

The major's eyes narrowed and he frowned, as if calculating whether to believe her or not. He sipped more tea. "Indeed," he said.

Of course, Mrs. Greenhow knew that she was playing with fire, or hot embers at the very least. It might only be a matter of time before she was arrested and locked away in the Old Capitol Prison. Would the Yankees dare to do such a thing? A few weeks ago, she never would have thought it would come to that. But once blood began to flow on the battlefield, she was sure that they might. She was more than willing to take the chance and do what she could for the South until that time came.

She poured the major more tea and smiled. They had crossed swords and riposted. She would try another line of attack. "Now tell me, what do you hear of General Scott's health? They say he has the gout, poor man."

CHAPTER SIXTEEN

ANNA NEVER HAD BEEN ONE TO BACK DOWN FROM ANYTHING. AS A woman in a man's world, she couldn't afford to. And truth be told, even Anna wasn't blind to the fact that her privileged background had imbued her with an arrogance that came from being a member of one of the South's first families.

Arrogance made for poor armor. For the first time, she began to realize the danger that she was in. That big Irishman Flynn had tried to warn her, and she could see now that he'd been right. She might even now be trapped like a busy spider in a web of her own spinning.

Her epiphany came in the form of a dead man swinging from a rope. The branch from which he was suspended creaked slightly because of the weight, but the ancient oak was otherwise silent, a brooding presence on the empty road. The quiet was like an admonishment. After all, any man who was in danger of being hanged should have seen to it that he wasn't caught in the first place. *If silence be good for the wise, how much better for fools*, she thought. A handful of local farmers had gathered and were debating whether to cut the man down.

She had taken a good look at the face. Unfortunately, she knew the man. She noted that his features were starting to swell in the heat and his tongue protruded grotesquely. She turned away.

"Looks like they hanged a spy," said the driver of the carriage that she had hired to carry her from Richmond to Washington—or at least, as close as she could get to Washington.

"A spy?" She looked around at the farmers. "Does anyone know what happened?"

"Devere's Legion hanged him when they was passing by, ma'am," said one of the locals. In a show of good manners, he took off his hat as he spoke to her. "They caught him nearby, trying to get across the Potomac. We heard he was found with secret papers on him."

"Secret papers?"

"A letter from a spy."

"Well, spy or not, the decent thing to do is to cut him down," she snapped.

"I'm not sure Colonel Devere and his cavalrymen would want that, ma'am."

"Do you see Colonel Devere here? I said to cut him down!"

"And just who are you, ma'am, if you don't mind me askin'?" The farmer suddenly seemed keenly interested in Anna. Manners forgotten, he put his hat back on. "The colonel said he was lookin' for a woman, said she was a spy, too."

"I am sure this woman is long gone, even if she really is a spy," Anna said.

"The colonel was certain she's a spy. I would imagine there's a reward."

"A reward! How ridiculous."

The farmer looked at his neighbor. "What was that woman's name that the colonel wanted?"

The other man shook his head. Anna was glad that he couldn't remember because her carriage driver knew her name.

Suddenly, it did not seem like a good idea to tarry any longer. The farmer had said that Colonel Devere and his cavalry were looking for a woman. Given that the letter carried by the man now hanging from the tree had been signed by Anna, she knew that Devere would be looking for *her*.

She had made two copies of the letter with the information that she had gathered in Richmond. She still planned to deliver the letter herself, but had sent the second copy ahead in case she was delayed. Considering that her messenger had been hanged, it was now up to her to get to Washington as soon as possible.

She turned to her driver. "We'll leave this poor man to these people in hopes that they do the right thing and cut him down and bury him. I want to reach Fredericksburg if possible before dark, and be across the Rappahannock in the morning."

"Yes, ma'am."

Anna climbed into the carriage and they rolled on. However, she was well aware that the group of farmers beneath the oak were staring after her curiously.

What if one of them rode ahead and managed to get a message to Devere in hope of a reward?

If that happened, she had no doubt that she would find herself swinging from the next suitable tree. She knew that Devere would show her no mercy.

She needed to focus her attention now on avoiding Devere and his legion at all costs. Unfortunately, it didn't help that the carriage was much too obvious.

She signaled the driver to stop.

"Ma'am?"

"Isn't there another way to go?" she asked.

"Maybe," he said doubtfully. "But those roads will be in rough shape. They'll bounce this carriage to pieces. It won't be a pleasant ride for you, ma'am."

"I don't care about that," she said. "Find another way to Washington." She almost added, *it's a matter of life and death.*

* * *

BY THE TIME that Devere's Legion arrived in northern Virginia, they were late to the party. Thousands of troops and even hundreds of spectators were already there, awaiting the battle that was sure to come.

In a sense, the battle was not so different from the duel that Flynn and Captain Blaine had fought. Both sides had agreed upon rules of engagement. Both sides felt that they had been wronged and their only resolution would come from combat. No real strategic objectives were involved. Even the railroad that ran through Manassas was hardly worth fighting over.

The thousands of Union troops that had crossed the Potomac into Virginia were not on their way to capture Richmond. General McDowell did not have the supply chain in place for that. Instead, his objective was to destroy the Confederacy's Army of the Potomac commanded by General Beauregard that had taken position around Manassas. (Later on, it would be a Union army that designated itself the Army of the Potomac.)

While the Confederate troops were certainly threatening the United States capital, it was not actually Beauregard's intention to sack Washington City. He didn't have a plan in place for anything that grand. His army was a gesture, the opening gambit in a civil war. Then again, if the Union army was routed, the Confederates might push on to occupy the streets of Washington.

None of this strategy mattered much to the ordinary soldiers on both sides. They were simply fighting for a cause they believed in. They would let the generals and the politicians sort out what it all meant.

Weary from their ride, the men of Devere's Legion arrived to help reinforce the Confederate troops already dug in along the banks of Bull Run, the creek that threaded its way through the Virginia countryside, eventually emptying into the Occoquan River, a tributary of the Potomac.

Devere was not pleased about the orders he received to dismount and help occupy the earthworks dug by Beauregard's men.

"We're cavalry, dammit, not infantry," Devere complained. Suddenly, all their weeks of training on horseback seemed to have been wasted.

But his complaints fell on deaf ears. General Beauregard and the other ranking officers had larger concerns than an unhappy colonel, even a rich one like Devere.

Devere's Legion had no choice but to send their horses to the rear and move into the trenches. They found themselves extending the flank of a regiment from North Carolina, who greeted them with high spirits.

"It's about time you horse soldiers showed up! Now you're goin' to see how real soldiers fight."

Colonel Devere ignored the catcalls. He had remained mounted, as was his prerogative as an officer. It was clear that he had no intention of climbing down into the earthworks.

Fortunately, there were no Union troops in sight, but for how long?

"Sir, you might want to get down off that horse," Flynn said quietly. "There's no sense drawing fire."

He had no real love for the colonel, but if a Union sharpshooter made him a target and could actually shoot straight, it would mean that Captain Blaine would be in command of the legion. Flynn couldn't think of anything that would be quite so disastrous—both for the regiment and for him, personally.

"See to your men, Lieutenant Flynn," Colonel Devere said. "I'm not getting in that damned trench."

"Yes, sir." Flynn turned away, not sure if Devere was brave or just a fool.

"All right, men," Captain Blaine said. "Spread out and watch the other side of that creek. When the Yankees come at us, it will be from that direction."

The cavalrymen were poorly equipped to defend the earthworks. Unlike the North Carolinians on their right, who carried long-range Enfield rifles, the cavalrymen were mostly armed with revolvers and shotguns, or short carbines that didn't have much range. The sabers that they had practiced with all spring and summer just got in their way as they navigated the trenches. The gorgeous plumes in the officers' hats got dirty.

"I don't understand why we're not on horseback," Jay grumped.

"That's the thing about being a soldier," Flynn said. "You'll never be asked to do the thing that makes sense, but you have to do it anyway."

"If you say so," Jay said. "But right now, we'd do more good with shovels than with swords."

Flynn looked around at the men near him. They had been placed at the very end of the line, where the earthworks began to peter out into grass. Flynn and his men found themselves at the extreme end of the Confederate flank. There was nothing beyond them and Washington now but the shallow waters of Bull Run—and possibly several thousand Union soldiers.

Again, he was reminded that the handful of men under his command were the misfits of Devere's Legion—latecomers or men who didn't have strong ties to the original members of Devere's Legion, who had mostly come from Devere's home county. He might be in the Confederate army almost by accident, and he might not be much of an officer—only Jay's quick thinking had gotten Flynn "promoted" upon joining the legion. But these were his men now. They looked tired and disheartened. He knew that now was not the time to pile on more complaints.

"Listen," he said. "It doesn't matter if we're on foot or on horseback. We're soldiers. We're here to fight, and that's what we'll do. I can tell you one thing. We're going to see plenty of action."

"There's no one over there," Jay said, gesturing toward the empty ground beyond Bull Run. "I don't see any Yankees."

"They're here, all right," Flynn said. "Thousands of 'em. They mean to fight, as do our troops. When that time comes, and it won't be long, do what you're told and remember that you might be fighting for Virginia, but in the end, you're fighting for the man on your left and the man on your right."

Jay and the others seemed to let that sink in. Then Jay nodded. "Yes, sir," he said.

* * *

As the afternoon stretched toward the long summer evening, long columns of Union troops approached. They marched in formation, several men across, then rapidly spread out across the field on the far side of Bull Run. Aside from their skirmish days earlier, they hadn't seen Union troops before—and definitely not in such numbers. Until that afternoon, the concept of the enemy had seemed vague. Now there they were, hundreds of blue-coated troops, within rifle range. The war suddenly seemed quite real.

For the Union troops, this was likewise their first time seeing the enemy in any real numbers. Flynn watched the officers trying to keep order, but it didn't stop a few hot-headed soldiers from taking potshots at Colonel Devere, who still refused to get off his horse.

They heard the occasional pop of a musket, then saw a distant burst of smoke. Another fat, lead bullet whined overhead.

"Either those Yankees can't shoot, or Devere lives a charmed life," Flynn muttered.

Soon, it was clear that the Union troops wouldn't be satisfied with taking potshots. Flynn watched them getting ready to do something meaningful, busy as stirred-up ants. Finally, a company of soldiers advanced toward the creek and splashed into the water.

He could see that the Yankees intended to flank them, or perhaps it was a diversion. The rest of the enemy troops might attack once the Confederate soldiers were busy fighting off the attack on their flank.

"Here they come, boys!" Flynn warned.

Having forded Bull Run, the Union company reformed, fixed bayonets, and began to advance in two orderly rows. The blue wall of soldiers approached, bayonets glinting in the hazy evening sun.

The Union troops had put out a few skirmishers and shots began to whine through the air. From the far shore, the firing had become more general. Colonel Devere was finally obliged to get down off his horse.

In the earthworks, the cavalrymen began firing, but it was really just a lot of noise. The Union troops still weren't in effective range.

Jay stood up to take better aim at the enemy, for all the good that his revolver would do at this range.

The bluecoats moved faster, coming at the double. A tall officer with an enormous handlebar mustache led them from the front, moving slightly to one side of his advancing troops. He carried a sword in one hand and a pistol in the other. He shouted an order. The first line of Yankees dropped to one knee.

"Get down!" Flynn shouted at Jay, who hadn't heard him in the general firing that had broken out.

In a well-orchestrated motion, both the standing and kneeling Union soldiers put their muskets to their shoulders. It was clear that they were about to fire a volley.

Flynn had seen this before, in Italy. He knew what a well-aimed volley could do, how men fell as if cut down by a scythe.

He ran at Jay, hoping to get there in time. He pulled him down just as both lines of Union troops fired their volley. A rolling clap of thunder filled the stream valley, followed by billowing smoke. Nearby, men screamed in pain and agony as bullets found their mark.

"Reload!" shouted the Union officer.

"Keep your head down, lad," Flynn growled, pulling himself off Jay.

Jay looked up at him, white-faced.

In an impressively short amount of time, the Union soldiers reloaded and prepared to fire another volley. With another long, rolling thunderclap of gunfire, the enemy unleashed another storm of lead at the men in the earthworks, whose own pistols and shotguns were ill-suited to fire back. One or two blue-coated soldiers had slumped to the ground, but several of the troopers from Devere's Legion now lay bleeding—or dead.

Flynn had to admit that the Union officer knew his business. The Southerners liked to say that the Union army was made up of fools and cowards, but this lone officer and his men had already proven them wrong. He'd likely have his men fire another volley or two, then rush in to finish off whatever was left of the legion with their bayonets. He might even manage to turn the entire Confederate flank.

Flynn decided that he'd had enough. He couldn't watch his men being cut to pieces when the battle had barely begun.

He jumped up and waved his sword. "Let's go, lads! Let's chase them back to Washington!"

CHAPTER SEVENTEEN

THE YANKEES WERE STILL RELOADING AS THE MEN OF THE LEGION poured out of the earthworks. Eager to fight, they screamed the rebel yell, the yips and keening wails carrying above the sound of gunfire.

Some of the Yankees had been quicker than the rest to reload, and they fired again, but it was not the concentrated volley fire that had been so devastating. Instead, the firing became more general. As the men of the legion closed the distance to the enemy, their revolvers now had an advantage with their faster rate of fire. Several blue-coated soldiers fell. And then like a pack of wolves, the Confederates were upon them.

Considering that the cavalrymen hadn't trained as infantry, they were more like brawlers. Waving their swords and pistols, they crashed into the Union troops.

Flynn didn't consider that he was fighting Union troops, fellow Americans. Raging, he only knew that he was fighting the enemy, fighting for the man on his left and the man on his right—just as he had told his lads they must do.

Flynn hacked about him with his sword. A stout bluecoat raised his rifle to parry the blade, but Flynn beat it aside and quick as a flash slashed at the man, who fell, screaming.

He knocked aside a bayonet that was thrust at him, then shot the man with the LeMat revolver. Something deep within him welcomed the fight. He might have been an Irish warrior spearing the Roman invaders, or better yet, the hated English.

His throat felt raw, and he realized that he'd been screaming the rebel yell along with the others. He hadn't even been aware of it.

All around Flynn, the legionnaires fought tooth and nail, bayonet against saber. He saw two soldiers engaged in a fistfight, gouging and punching at one another. Out of the corner of his eye, he spotted Jay dueling with an enemy soldier who seemed to be getting the upper hand. Flynn clubbed the Yankee in the side of the head with the heavy sword hilt. As the man fell away, Jay gave Flynn a quick nod, then whirled away, facing an attacker coming at him from another direction.

Another Union soldier finished reloading his rifle, managing to point it at Flynn and pull and trigger. Flynn ducked and felt the hot muzzle blast on his cheek, then shot the soldier in the chest.

The revolver was empty and there was no time to reload. He would have to rely on the sword from here on out.

A shadow fell across him and he spun to find the Union officer standing in front of him, sword at the ready. The man's eyes above the big beard were steady and appraising—no hatred or anger there, but no fear, either.

Flynn swung his sword, but the officer parried expertly. Flynn was a strong man, but there was nothing weak about the Union officer's arm.

He stepped back, waiting for Flynn to come to him. Flynn took his time, unwilling to fall into a trap. The two men circled one another.

"*Is lá maith é bás a fháil,*" the officer said. It's a good day to die.

Flynn was surprised that the man spoke Irish. He was fighting another Irishman.

"*Níl aon deifir orm,*" Flynn replied. I'm in no hurry.

Flynn attacked, feinting and then thrusting, but the move was clumsy. A cavalry saber was not meant for fencing. The Union officer parried easily, then lunged at Flynn, who twisted just in time, but not before the sword point cut a hole in his battered coat.

Flynn fell back and looked at his opponent, whose expression hadn't changed. This was no 90-day officer, Flynn decided. Like Flynn, the man must have been a soldier on another battlefield. The two squared off, looking for an opening.

Dimly, Flynn remained aware of the fighting around him. There was no telling how this might end. The two units were almost evenly matched. Some of the Virginia boys ran to join the fight and slowly but surely, the sheer number of gray warriors began to overwhelm the Union soldiers. Still, the brutal hand-to-hand combat continued, unrelenting.

Flynn raised his sword to attack again, but was knocked aside by a rushing horse. The Union officer disappeared into the fray. He looked up to see that the rider was Colonel Devere, sweeping through the mass of Yankees like an avenging angel, firing down with his revolver in one hand and his sword in the other.

Devere's arrival, along with the rest of the legion and the Virginia troops, quickly turned the tide. The Union soldiers melted away, at first one by one, but then in groups. They splashed back across Bull Run, some of them helping the wounded.

Flynn caught another glimpse of the Union officer that he had locked swords with. The man stood in the middle of the creek, directing his men across. Some had run for the creek and splashed across in a panic, but the Union officer managed to rally enough men to create a ragged skirmish line. They reloaded their guns and stood ready to give the Confederates a volley if they dared to advance.

But the men of the legion had their blood up. Several whooped and started running for the creek, oblivious that they were running right toward the waiting Union muskets. Even if the legion managed to overwhelm the skirmish line, they had no hope against the mass of Union troops beyond. One good volley and they would be blown away like dandelion seeds in a hurricane wind.

Colonel Devere saw the danger and called them back.

"Hold!" he shouted, his voice like a trumpet. He had blood on his sword. "Hold, I tell you! Let them go!"

To Flynn's relief, none of the massed Union troops on the far bank had advanced to join the fight, which had ended once the bluecoats withdrew. He realized that this has been nothing more than a bloody prelude—the real battle promised to begin tomorrow. The Confederate position would remain unchallenged for now.

* * *

AS HIS BATTLE FURY SUBSIDED, Flynn looked around for Jay. He saw him standing nearby, sword hanging at his side, a splash of bright red blood on his sleeve.

"Lad! Are you hurt?"

"Did you see how we made them run! Wasn't that something!"

"Let me see that arm."

Jay seemed to notice the blood for the first time. He held up his arm and inspected it. "I don't believe it's mine," he said.

Flynn had reached the same conclusion. "You're all right then," he said with obvious relief. "That was a hot fight."

He looked around, expecting to see the ground littered with bodies. It was true that there were a few, both blue and gray, that lay unmoving.

Despite the savage fighting, the butcher's bill on both sides had been light in the end. In addition to the handful of dead, there were maybe a dozen wounded legionnaires. Although the Union troops had retreated, not a prisoner was taken. The enemy had managed to carry away all their wounded, leaving only the dead behind.

Guiding his horse through the havoc, Colonel Devere's gaze fell on Flynn. His eyes narrowed. While there had been precious little choice, it was true that Flynn had launched the attack without orders. Joined by Captain Blaine, Devere began to head in Flynn's direction.

Flynn's actions might have saved the earthworks along Bull Run, but it was also true that the skirmish had left the legion bloodied. From the look in Devere's eye, Flynn was sure that there would be hell to pay.

Fortunately for Flynn, the fighting had not gone unnoticed. They were still picking up the pieces and tending to the wounded when half a dozen riders approached. Judging by the amount of gold braid on their sleeves and the fine uniforms, these were officers.

"What men are these?" the lead rider demanded, intercepting

Devere before he could reach Flynn. "I know these Virginians to your right, but not you, sir."

With a start, Flynn realized from the man's neatly trimmed goatee and Louisiana accent that this must be General Beauregard. The general could be forgiven if he wasn't sure which small unit occupied his flank. There were now thousands of Confederate troops along Bull Run and the legion was just a cavalry company.

"Why, this is Devere's Legion, sir," the colonel replied, snapping to attention and saluting. Like Flynn, he had guessed that this must be Beauregard.

"Who the devil are you?"

"I am Colonel Devere, sir."

"Ah, Colonel Devere, we meet at last! You are the one who outfitted this unit at his own expense," the general said. "You are a true patriot, sir! And a fighter! Your men fought like wildcats. I believe those Union troops might have turned our flank otherwise. Well done."

"Thank you, sir." Of course, the colonel had been given no choice but to join the fight after Flynn had launched the attack. Devere certainly didn't give Flynn any credit.

"But they are cavalry? Why are you dismounted?"

"Those were our orders, sir."

"Not anymore, they're not. In the battle tomorrow, I want you on your horses. I shall hold you in reserve. Imagine what a scare you shall put into the Yankees when Devere's Legion comes riding down upon them!"

At that, the general wheeled his horse expertly and rode on, his staff following in his wake. This was a general with style.

Despite their losses, Devere now seemed pleased. He sat taller in the saddle and a rare smile crossed his stern features. For all his posturing, he might have been worried about being accepted as a real officer, or that his self-financed troops were real cavalrymen, but now those fears had been put to rest. "You heard the general! Mount up!"

* * *

NOW THAT THEY had been pulled out of defending the earthworks along Bull Run, the cavalrymen of Devere's Legion were soon riding deeper behind the Confederate lines. There were only a few landmarks in the vicinity, mostly a few scattered farmhouses, hills, and bridges across Bull Run.

"What place is that?" the colonel asked his adjutant, pointing toward a lone farmhouse.

"I believe that is the McLean house, sir."

"That's just where General Beauregard wants us." After their brief meeting, Beauregard had sent Devere a courier with written orders.

Between the men who had been killed or wounded in that short, sharp fight to hold the earthworks, the ranks of the legion were already depleted. They rode with several riderless horses brought along behind them.

Those who had survived or who had gotten off with light wounds counted themselves lucky. Also, the festive atmosphere that had followed them most of the way from the outskirts of Richmond was now long gone. The bloody skirmish that they had found themselves drawn into had permanently changed the mood.

Devere was not content to let his men rest, even after the long ride from Richmond or the fight at Bull Run. He had patrols ride out to screen against enemy cavalry. He even volunteered his men as couriers, racing between headquarters and the various generals in the field until their horses were lathered in the July heat. Captain Blaine led a patrol down the smaller roads leading to Manassas, looking for Union cavalry.

If it was a fight the Yankees wanted, it was a fight they were going to get.

CHAPTER EIGHTEEN

ANNA'S MIND HAD BEEN RACING AS USUAL, A MILLION MILES AWAY. She was so deep in thought that she scarcely noticed the bumps and jolts of the carriage carrying her north through the Virginia country-side. She had instructed the driver to keep off the main thoroughfares and he was doing just that, although it made the journey that much rougher. She had little choice—it seemed that she was being hunted as a spy.

Anna would not have labeled herself as a spy, but only an interested party—a curious tourist into the heart of the Confederacy. She felt that the information that she had collected in Richmond would be useful to the Union cause. Now, she just had to make certain that it was delivered. Her courier had been caught and hanged, so it was up to her now.

Gradually, she noticed that the creaking and swaying of the carriage had stopped. Her thoughts returned to the present. In the distance, she thought that she heard occasional gunfire.

"What's happened? Why have we stopped?"

"This is as far as I can take you," the driver announced. He came to the carriage door and opened it for her.

"What do you mean that this is as far as you can take me?" she demanded. "We had an arrangement."

"I said that I would take you as far as I could, which is this far."

He had already unloaded her baggage, which consisted of a trunk and a portmanteau, and dumped it beside the narrow track they were traveling. They had come to an open place, and she saw that he meant to turn the carriage around. In the distance, she saw a great deal of smoke, individual trails reaching into the humid sky. It looked like the smoke from campfires. A lot of campfires.

An army must lay in their path. The question remained, was it the Confederate or Union army—or both? She knew that a battle was imminent. Was this the place?

"Where are we?" she asked.

"That there is Bull Run," the driver said, pointing to the overgrown banks of a nearby stream. "We ain't far from Manassas Junction."

"Do you mean to abandon me? What am I to do with my luggage?"

The man shook his head. "That don't concern me. This is as far as I go."

Anna looked him up and down. She didn't know the man, but had simply hired him from one of the Richmond stables. He wore a brown coat, trousers with a prominent patch, and worn shoes. Initially, she had taken his ragged clothes as a sign of humility. Now she saw that she was mistaken. The shabby clothes must be an indicator of a shiftless character. He looked too old to be a soldier and the stubble of a gray beard did not improve his appearance. Maybe the man just needed encouragement.

"I'll double your fee to get me as far as Alexandria," she said.

"A dead man ain't got much use for money," he pointed out. "They're about to fight a battle here."

"You suffer from a lack of courage, sir," she said.

"Don't push your luck," he said. "I want another ten dollars for the danger you put me in."

"I beg your pardon?"

"You can pay me, or I can take it from you."

Anna considered her options. She didn't feel any fear, but realized that she had to face the reality of her situation. She was utterly alone.

She carried a derringer in a pocket of her light traveling coat, but she preferred not to shoot anyone. Or did she?

The two of them stood in the road, glaring at one another. The predatory look in the driver's eye matched the look of cool appraisal in Anna's gaze.

Finally, Anna sighed. This standoff was getting tiresome. She reached into her pocket. Briefly, she touched the handle of the derringer, then closed her fingers around her purse instead. "All right, here's another ten dollars."

"Why, that's Confederate money!"

"That is what I have, unless I can interest you in a gently used portmanteau."

Grumbling, the driver snatched the money. He climbed back aboard the carriage and flicked the reins to get the horse moving. The horse was almost as shabby as the driver, but the army had snapped up all the decent horseflesh in Richmond. As the carriage made its wide arc and returned to the road, Anna was forced to move out of the way before she was run over.

She didn't bother to watch the carriage out of sight. Instead, she walked over to her luggage.

There was no hope of carrying her trunk, of course. The clothes and books within would have to be abandoned. However, she could manage the portmanteau. She picked it up by the wooden handles and started up the road toward the line of campfires.

She hadn't walked more than fifty yards when she heard hoofbeats coming toward her. There was no way she could know if they were Confederates or Union troops approaching. Remembering the sight of the hanged man, she slipped off the road and into the woods. Never one for fashion, she had opted for sensible traveling clothes rather than a more cumbersome hoop skirt. She pushed her way among the trees and underbrush, then held herself very still.

A small group of riders pounded past, wearing gray uniforms. They were clearly on patrol. The lead rider wore a red plume in his hat. With a start, she realized that it was Captain Blaine. The rest of Devere's Legion must be nearby, including Colonel Devere himself—the man who had pledged to hang her as a spy.

Anna held her breath as Captain Blaine reined his horse to a halt. He had found her trunk.

Quickly, he dismounted and rifled through the contents. "Women's clothes," he said, sounding mystified. "Why the devil would some woman leave her trunk along the road?"

One of the cavalry troopers pointed into the distance, where the carriage was still visible, about to round a bend in the narrow road. "Captain, maybe it fell off that carriage!"

"Let's find out," Captain Blaine announced. "What would a carriage be doing out here, anyhow?"

He swung lightly into the saddle and the patrol galloped off in a swirl of dust.

How long would it be before Captain Blaine caught up to the carriage and learned that the driver had left his passenger behind. A passenger named Anna Ella Carroll, who was also suspected of being a Union spy? Blaine would be back, hanging rope in hand.

Anna returned to the road, having abandoned the portmanteau in the woods. She couldn't be burdened by that. She had the clothes on her back and the packet of information in her pocket, and that would have to be enough. She hurried along the road with no real plan in mind, other than to put some distance between herself and Captain Blaine.

* * *

ANNA'S only hope was that night was coming on. With any luck, she could lose herself in the darkness. But Captain Blaine and his men would be searching the road for her. She had to get off it, and soon. Exhaustion was beginning to tug at her, and she felt enormously thirsty after all that running and walking since the carriage driver had so unceremoniously abandoned her.

The campfires were so close now that she could smell the woodsmoke and the smell of cooking food. She wasn't really hungry— it was too hot to eat, anyhow. But she was definitely thirsty.

She began to pass a few Confederate soldiers, but they were infantry, not the cavalry of Devere's Legion. They would be unlikely to know that she was suspected of being a spy. One or two of the men nodded at her politely or took off their hats, but paid her little attention otherwise. She was puzzled by that at first, but soon spotted a handful of other women in the vast bivouac. These women appeared busy carrying water or stirring something in a pot over one of the campfires. From their clothing, it was clear that these were women used to hard work

She found the sight oddly moving. These Southern women could not fight in the coming battle, but they had followed their men to the front to help where they could. It spoke of a determination that Anna realized she had not entirely accounted for in the packet of information she carried. She had noted troop strengths, production at the Tredegar Ironworks, the qualities of the various generals she met, but she had taken no real measure of the enemy spirit. Should she be all that surprised? They were Americans, after all—it was just that they happened to live south of the Potomac.

Hoping that she would be seen as an officer's wife and thus left alone, Anna held her head high and made her way through the encampment. She would have liked to walk right through to the Union lines, but she knew that wouldn't be possible. The summer dusk grew deeper and the campfires flickered more brightly. She would have no hope of finding her way in the dark.

"Can I help you, ma'am?"

She hadn't seen the officer approaching. He had materialized out of the gloom, looking down at her in concern from his saddle.

"I am ... well, it just so happens that I am looking for my husband." She paused, searching for a name. "Lieutenant Flynn."

"What unit is he with, ma'am?"

"He serves in Devere's Legion."

Despite the dusk, she saw the man nod with approval. "There's no better cavalry. Shall I guide you to them?"

"Oh no," Anna blurted. "I am sure I can find them."

"All right," he said, turning in the saddle to point behind him. "If you go in this direction just a little further, maybe a quarter of a mile, and ask for them, I am sure you will find Devere's Legion. But I would hurry, ma'am. It is getting dark. Some of our boys aren't the gentlemen that they should be."

She spotted a canteen hanging from the officer's saddle. "Might I trouble you for a drink of water?"

"Of course," the officer said, and handed down his canteen.

Anna didn't bother with a few small sips, but tilted back the canteen and drank down half of it.

The officer seemed concerned. "Are you sure you'll be all right? It's no trouble to take you to Devere's Legion."

"Thank you for your kindness, sir, but that won't be necessary," Anna handed back the canteen and pushed on past the mounted officer, heading in the direction he had indicated.

As soon as she was out of the officer's sight, she turned in the opposite direction. The last place she wanted to be was anywhere near Colonel Devere and his cavalrymen.

The ground rose, and at the top of the hill, she spotted a barn. No one seemed to be around, so she hurried toward it. She had no shelter, and with night coming on, the barn would have to do.

The barn doors were already open and she slipped inside. The interior smelled strongly of horses, but the animals were long since gone—probably pressed into service by the Confederate army. The heat trapped inside made the barn hotter than the night air, but at least she would be under a roof.

"Hello?" she called, but there was no answer.

Satisfied, she made her way to a corner of the barn and stretched out in the straw, suddenly exhausted. She took out the derringer and gripped it in her hand. The officer had warned her about ruffians and she had no patience for that.

Smiling to herself, she realized that she was a long way from the Metropolitan Hotel. No matter—right now the pile of straw felt as wonderful as a feather bed to her tired body.

Her plan was to awake at first light and make her way into the Union lines. Once she had reached the relative safety of being surrounded by Union troops, she could return to Washington City with the vital information that she carried.

* * *

ONLY WHEN DARKNESS finally began to fall around nine o'clock did the bulk of the legion have the opportunity to get some much-needed rest. But the summer nights were short and Devere promised them that they would be up again well before dawn. That gave Flynn and the others just a few hours to sleep.

"I don't think I've ever been so tired," Jay said, sliding from his saddle.

Flynn nodded. He knew exactly how Jay and the others felt.

"See to your horses, lads," Flynn said, a little unnecessarily. Some of the men had already stripped off the saddles and were rubbing down their mounts with rags or even handfuls of straw. The horses were hobbled and left to graze on the rich summer grass. For a cavalryman, his horse always came first. "Then get something to eat. Nobody sleeps on an empty belly."

The men had already grouped themselves into informal messes, but there would be no real cooking tonight. A few men built small fires to heat water for coffee. It was a beverage that no soldier wanted to do without, no matter how tired he felt. The version that they brewed involved crushing coffee beans—often with the butt of a musket or revolver—dumping them into a metal pot full of water taken from Bull Run, adding a generous handful of sugar, and boiling it all into a brew so thick you could almost stand a spoon in it.

What Flynn preferred at the moment was whiskey. He had a bottle hidden away in his saddlebags and took a long pull, and then another, welcoming the bite of the liquor. He handed the bottle around. "Two pulls each, and no more. We need you fresh in the morning."

"Yes, sir."

They still had the bounty from their ride through Virginia—corn-bread, ham sandwiches, even a few early peaches.

"Save something for breakfast," Flynn reminded them. "You'll need it. Tomorrow promises to be another long day."

"I'm almost too tired to eat, anyway," Jay said, after he had wolfed down a chunk of cornbread slathered in butter, chased down with hot coffee.

For most of the men, Flynn included, their bed for the night would be a blanket, with a saddle for a pillow. The only exception was Colonel Devere. A group of men, weary though they were, had been detailed to erect a canvas tent for him.

As second in command, Captain Blaine made do with a sheet of canvas stretched over a tree limb. It would be enough to keep the nighttime dew off.

If Devere was angry with Flynn for launching the attack earlier, it hadn't stuck. After all, the colonel had been glad enough to accept the praise for their actions from General Beauregard.

As the men finished their meager dinner and rolled themselves into their blankets, Flynn said, "Lads, I'm proud of what you did today. That was a wicked fight."

"Those Yankees were tougher than I reckoned they would be," said one man.

Flynn nodded. He was thinking about the steadfast Union officer who had managed to keep control of his men even when they retreated. "They are just as determined as you are, in their own way."

"But we sure showed 'em today!" Jay said.

Flynn reached down and tousled the young soldier's hair. "That we did, lad. And we'll be sure to do it again tomorrow, so get some sleep."

Soon, the camp fell quiet as men fell upon their blankets. A few began to snore.

Flynn stayed awake for a bit, not quite ready for sleep, tired though he was.

The night was far from silent. After all, thousands of troops were spread across the countryside. It might be his imagination, but he could almost hear the tramping feet of Union soldiers on the Warrenton Turnpike. He could definitely hear the sound of crickets and a restless mockingbird, serenading the soldiers who had invaded the countryside. In some distant campfire, someone was playing a fiddle and singing.

Somewhere out there, he thought, Miss Carroll must be trying to make her way back to Washington. Just before dark, Captain Blaine had ridden into camp with news that he had found Miss Carroll's carriage, but no sign of the woman herself. Flynn had hoped that she would have had the good sense to give Manassas a wide berth, but that had been too much to hope for. No matter—that woman was no longer his problem, although he wished her well. She might be foolish, but she was brave enough.

Fireflies winked and sparked, mixing among isolated campfires that stretched as far as he could see in every direction. Darkness settled ever so slowly across the fields and woods.

All these men hadn't come here just to camp. When morning came, the battle would be engaged.

He recalled the fear he had felt upon seeing the blood on Jay's sleeve. While it had turned out that the blood wasn't Jay's, it was a reminder of the hard thing that an officer must do, which was to send his men into battle—even the men who were hardly more than boys. He had always envied officers, but now he wasn't so sure that the job was as easy as it looked.

Finally, Flynn rolled himself in his blanket and slept like the dead.

CHAPTER NINETEEN

GENERAL BEAUREGARD'S PLANS TO LAUNCH AN ATTACK ON THE Union lines and chase the enemy troops out of Virginia had been dashed when it was the Yankees who went into action first. By two o'clock in the morning, the Union soldiers were up and moving into position. Some of them hadn't slept at all since rushing from Washington City and now there promised to be another very long day before them. Adding to the displeasure of many was the fact that it was now Sunday morning.

If Flynn had been awakened by thunder the previous day, this morning it was actual cannon and musket fire that roused him.

By daybreak, the Union troops had opened fire, advancing against the Confederate lines. Caught by surprise and facing almost overwhelming numbers, the gray-clad troops began to fall back.

"Is the enemy attacking?" Jay asked in alarm.

"Aye, lad, that's why they're here. Someone had to throw the first punch."

Jay scratched some straw out of his hair. "You know what else? It's Sunday. Fighting on the Lord's Day just doesn't seem right somehow. Back home, we'd be going to church this morning."

Flynn laughed and clapped Jay on the shoulder. "Why settle for church when you can go to heaven instead?"

Jay gulped. "I'm not sure that makes me feel any better."

The Union attack had left the Confederates feeling wrong-footed. In their own minds, they were the ones who would be attacking, not the other way around. The high spirits in the Confederate camp gave way to uneasiness. In the dim morning light, it was impossible to tell just how many enemy troops they were facing. From the shouts and the crashing roll of volley fire, it was clear that this was no skirmish. The Union troops were attacking in force.

* * *

FOR ANNA, it seemed as if she had just fallen asleep in the barn when she was awakened by a deep booming sound. She thought at first that it was thunder, but then realized that she must be hearing cannons firing. She couldn't be certain, but she guessed from the direction that the noise was coming from that these were Union cannons.

Her heart sank. If the battle had already started, it would be that much more difficult to make her way into the Union lines. But at the same time, another part of Anna felt a thrill. The war had truly begun. Like most Americans, she thought that the war promised excitement. She had yet to see the carnage that those anonymous guns in the night could cause.

She had no water for washing or anything to eat, so she simply combed the straw out of her hair with her fingers. It was still too dark to see anything, so she waited in the barn until streaks of the coming dawn began to light the eastern sky. At least morning came early in July.

From the barn on top of the higher ground, she had a good view of the Confederate camp below. There was no time this morning for cooking fires. Instead, the men had been rousted from sleep and into action. She heard shouts, the clank of harnesses and bridles, and the tramp of marching feet. As the light grew, she could make out the regiments moving into action.

When she could see well enough, she left the barn and walked in the direction that the troops were taking.

She came across an officer on horseback—relieved to see that he was not one of Devere's Legion, and asked him what was happening. "Has the battle begun, sir?"

The officer seemed startled by the appearance of a woman. "Good God, ma'am! What are you doing out here?"

"I came to see the battle and I got lost," she said, which was as good of an excuse as any that she could think of.

"The Federals have attacked all along Bull Run," he said. "It's not safe here, ma'am. You need to go back."

"I will, and thank you, sir."

She waited until the officer had rushed off, then continued toward the sound of fighting.

Off to her left, a shell exploded overhead, not far from a group of riders. A horse screamed and one of the riders toppled to the grass and did not get back up. For the first time, a cold fear seeped through her. The war was no longer so abstract.

Another shell exploded, even closer this time. The noise was ear-splitting. Out in the open, Anna felt exposed. She began to run for the nearby woods, thinking that the trees would offer some shelter.

In between the bursting shells, she heard another sound. Something zinging through the air, almost like angry bees. Bullets, she realized. Anna ran faster.

Panting, she reached the edge of the woods. More shells exploded. One or two hit the earth and raised clods of dirt and grass. She saw another man fall not more than fifty feet away. All that she could think to do was to get off that field. She picked up her skirts and ran harder for the trees.

* * *

It wasn't long before Devere's Legion was called into action. Flynn and the others joined the entire legion, which was assembling in a field as the morning sun peeked over the horizon, lighting the sky in brilliant shades of orange, red, pink, and blue. It reminded Flynn of the mother of pearl iridescence of an oyster shell. Nature had a cruel way of making life seem all the sweeter and fleeting when it hung in the balance. He wondered how many men wouldn't live to see that sun go down this day.

"To arms, men, to arms!" Captain Blaine shouted as he rode up and down the lines of cavalrymen. He only stopped so that Colonel Devere could address the legion.

"This is the battle that will settle the war," Devere proclaimed. "Whatever happens today, make me proud, make your families and wives and sweethearts proud, make Virginia proud!"

The men cheered and whooped, adding to the growing noise that morning. Unlike Colonel Devere, Flynn thought that it might take more than one battle to settle the war, but he had to admit that the man gave a stirring speech.

Minutes later, they were riding toward the sound of the guns. The horses nickered and whinnied in excitement. Spurs jangled and sabers clanked. Already, most of the men were sweating in the heat, rivulets running down their faces. It promised to be a long, hot day.

Devere and Blaine rode at the front of the column, leading the men toward the sound of the fighting. General Beauregard had planned to launch an attack from his position of strength in the earthworks along Bull Run, surprising the Union troops and attacking their flank. But General McDowell had made the bold move to cross Bull Run at Sudley Springs Ford and launch a full attack against the center of the Confederate line.

It was more than just a blunt attack. Instead, McDowell's troops feinted not once, but twice, prompting Beauregard to pull troops in and meet the assault. Meanwhile, McDowell's real target was the Confederate flank. Soon, the Confederates found themselves racing to reinforce section after section of their line and confusion mounted. Forced from their dug-in positions, the Confederates fell back from Bull Run to Matthews Hill.

Working against General Beauregard was the fact that his forces remained outnumbered. Desperately, he hoped that General Johnston's men would arrive from the Shenandoah Valley. Johnston only had about nine thousand men, but the arrival of fresh troops could turn the tide of battle.

For now, all that the surprised and outnumbered Confederate army could do was fight—and hope that luck turned in their favor—and victory along with it. Nearly all of the men and officers, not to mention all the civilian spectators, believed that the outcome of this single battle would decide the war. The troops of the victorious side would soon be marching to seize Washington—or Richmond—and the war would be over.

Devere's Legion was soon caught up in the confusion that had come over the Confederate army. They raced from one place in the line to another, only to discover that it was yet another Union feint. Meanwhile, Union troops massed on the flank.

For Colonel Devere and his men, this confused mess was not the battle that they had envisioned. Devere's dream was to lead his men in a glorious charge that would sweep the enemy from the field and win the day. Ships and streets might be named for him someday, just as they had been named for the heroes of the Revolutionary War. By noon, it seemed too much to hope for.

"Just give us someone to attack, damn you!" Colonel Devere shouted in frustration at yet another courier ordering him to some new point on the battlefield. His men and horses were hot, tired, and dusty, and they had yet to fight anyone—all that they had done was ride from one false alarm to another.

But then came their chance. By now, the Confederate army clung to the high ground around the Henry farmhouse. If they were pushed from that hill, the battle might very well be over, and the war would be lost.

Weakened, the Confederate line fell back. Several officers had fallen and the men had no leaders for the moment. Some started to turn toward the rear. It was not a full retreat, but it was clear that the Southern line was beginning to crumble.

The Union troops seemed to sense opportunity and advanced into the gap. At the foot of the hill, a regiment began to advance with fixed bayonets. The Union battle cry was nothing like the weird, keening wail of Confederate troops. Instead, it was something deep and guttural. This was the sound that came now from several hundred Union soldiers intent on finishing the rebellion for good. They seemed to have a clear path up the gentle slope. Once the Confederates were pushed off this hill, they might have a clear road to Richmond.

For once, no courier appeared, but Devere didn't need orders. It was plain to see what needed to be done.

"Get ready, lads," Flynn said in a low voice to the men around him. "Use your revolvers and when you get in close, use your swords. They'll fire a volley or two at us, but don't let them reload. Ride them down."

"What do you mean?" Jay wondered.

"We're going to charge, lad, that's what."

Flynn was proven right when Captain Blaine shouted for the men to prepare themselves. They drew their weapons and loosed their swords in their scabbards.

Colonel Devere raised his sword and his beautiful, black stallion reared up eagerly. A bugle sounded. The colonel pointed his sword and shouted, "Charge!"

In a flowing wave, the cavalry swept down the hill toward the enemy.

For one glittering moment, the Yankees' path to smashing the Confederate line had been clear. Victory was just beyond the points of their bayonets. But now that gap in the line had been filled by cavalry, sweeping down the hillside toward the Union troops.

Flynn had been right that the Union troops would fire a volley. From horseback, he saw the stabs of flame and roiling smoke, followed almost instantly by the ragged thunder of massed musket fire. He hunkered low on the bay roan's neck and heard a ball or two whistle past. A handful of riders fell from their saddles and a horse screamed and tumbled, bringing its rider down with it. Fortunately for Flynn and the rest, there was a natural tendency to aim too high when firing uphill. Most of the bullets ended up flying over their heads.

Now, the blue-coated soldiers scrambled to reload, but there was no time for that as the riders pounded toward them. One or two Union officers fired their pistols. Another cavalryman tumbled from the saddle, but there was no stopping the avalanche of gray riders flowing down the slope.

It was curious that, unlike in Europe, infantrymen were not trained in the use of the square as a tactic to defend against cavalry. Even in his brief stint as a soldier in Italy, Flynn had learned the rudiments. Infantry quickly learned to form a four-sided square, the front row kneeling, bayonets facing out, as a way to repel horsemen. It was a highly effective tactic that European infantry had learned as a defense against Napoleon's savage cuirassiers.

But the Union troops had nothing like that. Some frantically tried to ram another cartridge into their muskets while others raised their bayonets, but there was no concerted effort at defense.

Then the horsemen were upon them. Flynn's big bay roan crashed into the Union line, knocking down soldiers. He saw a terrified young soldier curl himself into a ball as Flynn's horse rode over him.

Flynn held his fire, although he had the LeMat revolver in his right hand and the reins in his left. He realized that he didn't want to shoot any more Yankees than necessary—unless they shot at him. His battle rage from the previous day had dissipated. He hoped that the horses would be enough to scatter them.

He sawed at the reins to turn his horse away as a bluecoat plunged toward him, wielding a bayonet. Another horse crashed into the man, sending him spinning away. Flynn realized that it was Jay, who held his sword ready, but also seemed reluctant to use it. He was letting the momentum of his horse scatter the enemy instead.

The rest of the horsemen had no compunctions about using their swords and pistols. From horseback, they fired down at the Union soldiers. When their guns were empty, they used their swords. Captain Blaine spurred through the bluecoats, hacking down with his saber. A cavalry saber was a wicked instrument. With its heavy, slightly curved blade, it smashed through flesh and bone. Bluecoats fell screaming in Blaine's wake. Not far away, Colonel Devere was employing his sword in much the same way, swinging it again and again at the swirling confusion of bluecoats. He had lost his hat somewhere, so that his long hair flew wildly, making him look more than a madman than a Virginia gentleman. Screams and curses filled the air.

One soldier ran from the melee, making a dash back toward Bull Run—maybe even hoping to run all the way back to Washington.

Captain Blaine spotted him and rode him down, dropping the soldier with a savage swipe from his saber. Flynn caught a glimpse of Blaine's face and saw how it was twisted into a rictus of battle madness. With a shout, Blaine rode back into the fray.

Flynn holstered his pistol and drew his sword. It was true that some ran, but other Union soldiers were fighting back with the desperation of wounded, cornered animals. He looked around, but had lost sight of Jay in the confusion.

Flynn focused his attention on fending off the bayonets that jabbed at him and the bay roan, keeping the horse moving to make a difficult target. He felt the horse stumble once or twice and had the uneasy realization that they were trampling on the Union dead and wounded.

The charge had spread out like a spill, giving more space between the riders. The remaining Union soldiers were shot, slashed, or ridden down. A bluecoat tried to surrender, but Captain Blaine ignored the man's raised hands and slashed him across the face. The soldier reeled away, screaming. Another cavalryman rode up and shot the soldier in the back, finishing him.

The riders spent another minute or two viciously dealing with any bluecoat survivors in similar fashion. A few escaped to spread the story of what they were calling the Dark Horse Cavalry. But it was soon clear that the field belonged to Devere's Legion. The threat to the Confederate line had ended.

The victorious charge hadn't come without a price. Several riderless horses milled about, but he could still see Blaine, Devere, and Sergeant Creighton on horseback. They seemed to have come through the fight unscathed.

Flynn looked around for Jay, but the young cavalryman was nowhere in sight. Where the devil had he gone?

CHAPTER TWENTY

ELSEWHERE ON THE BATTLEFIELD, THE TIDE WAS ALSO TURNING against the Union troops. General McDowell had come so close to victory. The early morning surprise attack and the fighting throughout much of the afternoon had given the Union most of the momentum. It was becoming clear to most observers that the battle was only McDowell's to lose. The advance by the Union regiment into the gap in the Union lines would have clinched the deal.

But the arrival of Devere's Legion had changed the momentum of the battle. Near the top of Henry House Hill, a former professor from the Virginia Military Institute rallied the troops under his command, even as the Union fought hard to capture the hill.

"There is General Jackson, standing like a stone wall!" cried another general named Bernard Bee, a career army officer from Charleston. "Rally behind the Virginians!"

His troops followed the example being set by Jackson just when it was needed most to stand firm against the Union onslaught. General Bee soon fell mortally wounded while leading his troops, hit by shrapnel, but General "Stonewall" Jackson and his Virginians held the line.

Running up against a determined enemy, the Union attack began to falter. After all, many of them had marched the twenty-five miles from Washington and gone into action without any rest or sleep. There hadn't been time for a decent meal. Their feet were blistered inside their hobnailed brogans. Their wool uniforms grew brutally hot as the July sun beat down. Their mouths tasted of gunpowder from ripping open paper cartridges and their throats burned from the sulfurous smoke. All in all, the Union troops were tired, hungry, and thirsty after hours of unrelenting marching and fighting. Now here stood the Virginians, resolute. Everyone from their officers to the newspapers had promised them that the rebels would run at the first sound of gunfire. But here they stood. It began to be too much.

Still, the Union had the advantage of artillery. Several batteries pummeled the enemy with solid shot and even grapeshot, which was a canister filled with iron balls that wrought gruesome devastation at close range. The hill was becoming covered with Confederate dead and wounded.

Determined though they might be to seize the hill, the Union artillery was tearing them to shreds.

* * *

HAVING EXPENDED their energy in such a glorious charge, Devere's Legion found itself guarding the rear of the Confederate position. There was still no sign of Jay, and Flynn was worried.

"Have you seen young Warfield?" he asked one cavalryman after another, when Jay still hadn't turned up with other stragglers.

"The last I saw of him, he was with a group of riders chasing after some of those Yankees," said Tyler, the adjutant.

"Didn't they come back?"

Tyler shook his head. "I saw them ride out, but I lost track of them."

"Dammit all!" Flynn shook his head. This wasn't good news. While the cavalrymen had stopped the Union advance, more bluecoats had already been streaming toward the hill. It was possible that Jay and the others had been cut off, like the tide coming in and leaving clamdiggers stranded on a sand bar.

Flynn's mind raced. Had Jay been trapped or captured? Had he been wounded or killed? Silently, he cursed the lad for chasing after the retreating Union troops. It had been a battle, not a fox hunt.

There was no time to ride out and look for him. Giddy from the success of the charge, Colonel Devere was already spoiling for more action. He had his sights set on routing the Union artillery that was pummeling the Confederate position on Henry House Hill.

"Are you sure, sir?" Captain Blaine asked, expressing his doubts. "Surely their canister fire would cut us down before we could reach them."

"They may be able to fire at us once or twice, but we won't give them time to reload," Devere promised.

"But do we have any orders to do that, sir?" Blaine did not sound convinced. "We have been ordered to guard the rear."

"Orders be damned! Do you think Marshal Ney waited for orders? Or Francis Marion?"

Flynn glanced in Blaine's direction, and the two men exchanged a look. For once, they seemed to agree on something. Devere's plan was foolhardy, to say the least. New to war or not, the Union gunners had quickly learned their business. Their guns would easily sweep riders from the field like a shotgun blasting a flock of crows from the sky.

Flynn spoke up. "Beggin' the colonel's pardon, but charging the guns does sound foolhardy, sir. The legion has already lost twenty or thirty men in this fight. Can we stand to lose more? Charge those guns and we'll be down to half strength—or worse."

Devere glared at him. "Some might call that cowardly advice."

"Look at those guns, sir." Flynn pointed in the direction of the battery, where another gun fired. A smoke ring boiled out from the cannon's muzzle as it delivered another solid shot into the Confederate ranks. "Do you want to lose half the legion?"

"If I want your advice I shall ask for it, *Lieutenant* Flynn," Devere said.

Flynn sighed. "Yes, sir."

Fortunately, the discussion had bought them time. An infantry regiment was already moving into position to attack the enemy artillery.

"Are those boys theirs or ours?" someone asked.

"Why, that's the 33rd Virginia," someone said. "At least, I think it is."

The confusion came from the fact that the infantry wore blue uniforms, even though they fought for the Confederate army. This early in the war, there still wasn't a standardized uniform, resulting in what was sometimes an array of various styles of uniforms, in different shades. More than a few troops that fought for the Confederacy wore blue uniforms and some Union troops wore gray. They had to be identified by their unit flags, which wasn't easy to do on a smoke-covered battlefield.

The cavalrymen weren't the only ones who were debating which side the infantrymen were on. As the infantry advanced toward them, the Union artillery fell silent.

"Hold your fire!" an artillery officer shouted. "They're wearing blue. Those must be our men!"

Moments later, it became clear how wrong he'd been. Having nearly reached the artillery, the blue-coated soldiers charged the last fifty feet. They stormed among the guns, firing their muskets at point-blank range, wielding their bayonets, and driving off or capturing the Union artillerymen. Whether it had been an intentional ruse or not, the confusion over the color of the uniforms had cost the Union its well-placed batteries, strengthening the Confederate army's hold. Virginia artillerymen were rushed into place, and the guns were turned toward the Union troops.

This one incident alone might not have been enough to win the battle. But as the fortunes of war would have it, this was not the worst that was befalling General McDowell's army as the afternoon grew late. The Union troops were growing exhausted. McDowell had already committed his reserves. There were no more troops to send. Meanwhile, reinforcements were arriving for the rebels.

Fresh Confederate troops under Jubal Early were now pouring onto the battlefield. They had ridden the train up from the Shenandoah Valley. It was the first time on any battlefield in the world that troops had arrived on a battlefield by rail, rather than on horseback or on their own two feet. They marched directly from the train to the battlefield.

These thousands of Confederates had originally been stationed around Harpers Ferry, but had given Union troops there the slip, only to reappear in the nick of time at Manassas. If it had been part of the Confederate strategy, the arrival of the reinforcements would have been a stroke of military genius. But as it was, the fresh troops were mainly a result of luck and timing.

Still, it was enough. All across the battlefield demoralized Union troops began to pull back. The tired, exhausted men didn't have any fight left in them. They were all worn out. Some dropped their muskets and walked away. Even more egregious was the fact that some 90-day units decided that their term of service had expired. Whole regiments walked off the battlefield—never mind that there was still much fighting to be done.

To prevent an overall collapse, General McDowell gave the order to withdraw. What had seemed like certain victory just hours before was now a rout.

The Union troops were not alone in wanting to leave the field of battle, now that a Northern victory looked unlikely. Hundreds of civilians had taken up positions wherever there was a vantage point to observe the battle. The picnic atmosphere had long since evaporated at the sight of so much carnage. Horrified, many had already left and turned their carriages for Washington.

But others had been too engrossed by the combat to have the good sense to flee. Still more were politicians who felt the need to support the troops, or relatives whose brothers, sons, and fathers were among the combatants. Anxiously, they had hung about the battlefield, hoping for some word about their relatives' fate.

Almost all of the spectators were from Washington, even if some secretly cheered on the rebels. Richmond was too far away for spectators to make a day of it.

Now, these crowds of civilians were also leaving, joining the stream of soldiers flowing back toward the Union capital.

At first, as afternoon stretched toward evening, the retreat was orderly enough. If the Union troops wanted to leave, the Confederates seemed content to let them go—at least at first. A few officers realized that this was the Confederacy's opportunity to crush the Union army for good in one decisive battle. Already, some talked of invading the streets of Washington.

With their eye on complete victory over the Union, these officers took action. Captured artillery was repositioned yet again to fire at the retreating troops. Shells exploded in the roadside trees and solid shot skipped across the fields, terrifying the civilians who had put themselves in harm's way by driving out to witness the battle. This was far more than they had bargained for when packing their picnic baskets early that morning.

* * *

NOT KNOWING what else to do, Anna had stayed hidden in the woods, watching regiments rush past toward the battlefront. She was not one to cower, but neither was she a fool. She had no idea where she was or what was happening. The smart thing to do seemed to be to stay put. Her stomach rumbled, but that was the last of her worries, given that she could still hear the zing of stray bullets.

Worse yet was her thirst. She hadn't had a drink of water since availing herself of that officer's canteen the night before.

From her hiding spot in the woods, Anna could see the body of the soldier who had been hit by shrapnel. His canteen was clearly visible. The sun rose higher and the heat grew.

Was she desperate enough to take the dead soldier's canteen filled with water? The other troops that she could see were far away now and the firing seemed to have slackened.

Anna stepped out of the woods and walked over to the dead man. She could see a gash in his chest where the shrapnel must have hit him. Mercifully, it appeared that he had died instantly. His face was bearded and his mouth hung open. His eyes stared sightlessly.

Anna had always been a woman of words and ideas. More than ever, she realized that ideas had consequences. The men who had argued for dividing the nation had gotten what they wanted. The result was this dead young man in the Virginia grass.

His musket lay nearby, but that was of no use to her. All that she wanted was a drink of water. She reached down for his canteen, but he had pinned the strap under him when he fell. With an effort, she worked the strap out from beneath him. She looked around, but no one seemed to be paying any attention to her. The last thing she wanted anyone to think was that she was looting the dead.

With the canteen in hand, she returned to the woods. It did not seem safe to go any further than retrieving the canteen at the moment. The water was warm from being in the summer sun, but it tasted more wonderful than the best wine.

More troops rushed into action, more than she had seen before. Were these reinforcements? As the afternoon grew long, she heard soldiers whooping.

"They've broken, boys! The Yankees are running!"

Could it be that the Union had lost the battle? Now more than ever, the documents that she carried seemed of utmost importance. She had to get back to Washington. The firing had decreased to a smattering of musket shots and cannon fire. Now was her chance.

Anna made her way toward where the worst of the fighting had taken place. The carnage amazed her. Dead men lay strewn across the fields and along the banks of the creek. She tried to ignore them and pushed on until she reached the Union lines.

But already, they were falling back, leaving the field to the Southerners. She fell in with the stream of troops and civilians moving along the road toward Alexandria. For better or for worse, she had joined the retreat.

* * *

STILL ITCHING FOR A FIGHT, Colonel Devere readied his cavalrymen to ride out and harass the retreating Union forces.

"To me, men! Our duty is not over yet."

Flynn had no choice but to go with them, but what he really wanted to do was look for Jay. As far as he could tell, the battle was over. The Confederate army had carried the day. But Colonel Devere did not see it that way.

"Look after your men, Lieutenant Flynn. We are riding after the Yankees to finish them off, once and for all!"

Captain Blaine may have been reluctant to ride against the Union artillery earlier, but he was more than enthusiastic about harassing the enemy retreat. "Carry two guns if you can," he exhorted the men. The expression on his face was almost gleeful. "When we get in among them, cut down all that you can with your sabers."

Flynn was not as eager. "We should let them go if we can," he said, then muttered, "*The quality of mercy is not strained. It droppeth as the gentle rain from heaven.*"

"What's that?" Blaine wondered, having overheard him.

"Nothing, Captain." Flynn could see that both Devere and Blaine had their blood up. Now was not the time to argue with them, but he would keep his sword sheathed. He'd been quoting Shakespeare again. It was just a shame that Jay wasn't here to appreciate it. The lad's absence still worried him.

Flynn turned to the men around him. "By all rights, this battle should be over, lads. Just remember that you've already done your part, just as those Union men have."

A few of the men nodded. They saw things the same way. But many more were eager to load their guns and make sure that their swords were loose in their scabbards, intent on eliminating a few more Yankees.

With Colonel Devere at the head of the column, the legion rode out to bring destruction down on the heads of the retreating troops.

It didn't take long to cross out of the Confederate lines and find the line of retreat. What they found there was pandemonium.

McDowell's troops were too green to maintain order for long and most of his officers did not have the experience to oversee an orderly withdrawal. To make matters worse, there was only one road leading away from the battlefield. Thousands of troops crowded onto the Warrenton Pike, streaming toward the Cub Run Bridge across Bull Run, headed in the direction of Centreville, Fairfax Courthouse, and then Alexandria and Washington City beyond.

There was little room to maneuver on the road as it became jammed with exhausted men, walking wounded, wagons, horses, and even artillery. They ignored commands from the few officers who had the good sense to try and maintain some order.

In the confusion, a supply wagon had overturned on the road, adding to the bottleneck. Civilians were mixed among the soldiers. Several men were trying to untangle the horses from the harness and then heave the wreck off the road, but it was taking precious time.

At the head of the Dark Horse Cavalry, Devere reined to a halt.

Up ahead, a woman walked down the middle of the road. This in itself was unusual, because the vast majority of civilians and soldiers fleeing down the road were men. She did not seem to be in any hurry to get out of the way of the approaching cavalry.

"Clear the way, damn you!" Devere shouted.

The woman turned and looked back at the Confederate troops. Her eyes narrowed as she glared back at the colonel with a look of disdain. She put one hand on her hip, indicating that she had no intention of moving. This was not a woman who took orders from anyone.

A moment later, her eyes widened in recognition. The colonel, too, had recognized the woman blocking the road.

"You!" he shouted.

Flynn had ridden forward as soon as Devere brought the column to a halt. There was something familiar about the haughty stance of the woman in the road. Astonished, he saw that it was Miss Carroll.

Devere raised his pistol.

Miss Carroll hitched up her skirt and ran for the woods bordering the road.

The colonel fired. He seemed to deliberately aim to frighten Miss Carroll because his bullet only kicked up the dirt at her feet. She kept running.

Devere holstered his revolver. "Dammit! I won't shoot a woman in the back, but I will see her hanged. Captain Blaine, bring that woman to me! She's a spy!"

"What about the Yankees, sir?"

"I will lead the legion against the enemy. You see to that woman."

"Yes, sir."

Captain Blaine looked none too pleased about having to break off his ride to glory to go after Miss Carroll. He reined forward, clearly intending to cut Miss Carroll off before she reached the trees.

Flynn just watched, telling himself that Miss Carroll wasn't his concern anymore.

Or was she?

Cursing under his breath, Flynn rode after Captain Blaine.

CHAPTER TWENTY-ONE

FLYNN HEARD DEVERE SHOUTING AT HIM TO COME BACK, BUT HE ignored the colonel. Devere gave up and rode on with the rest of the legion, intent on attacking the retreating Union troops from the rear.

Flynn spurred the horse forward, amazed at how much ground Blaine and Miss Carroll had already covered. Still, Blaine was on horseback and had nearly caught up to her.

"Stop, damn you!" Blaine shouted.

His horse was close enough that she must be able to feel the animal's hot breath. Blaine leaned forward and stretched out one arm, ready to snatch her by the back of the neck.

But Miss Carroll did not so much as look back before she ran headlong into the trees, forcing her way through the thick wall of brush at the boundary, fighting through a tangle of blackberries and pokeweed. Blaine's horse reared, refusing to follow Miss Carroll into the wall of vegetation. The captain had been off-balance, ready to snatch up his quarry, and he tumbled from the saddle and fell headlong into the greenery.

Miss Carroll was gone. Thorns had caught at her dress and ripped bits of cloth away, leaving them hanging among the blackberry canes. She had disappeared into the dense, dusky woods.

Flynn came riding up just as Blaine was getting on his feet again, cursing as he extricated himself from the blackberry thorns.

"What the devil are you doing here?" Blaine demanded.

"The colonel sent me to help," Flynn lied.

"I don't need any help to catch that bitch," he said.

Flynn grinned down at him. "Are you sure now, Captain? It looks to me like Miss Carroll has gotten the better of you."

Blaine's hand went to his revolver. Flynn did the same. The two men stood glaring at each other. It was the duel all over again.

Slowly, Blaine lowered his hand. "Fine," he hissed. "But after we find this woman and hang her, I think it goes without saying that the two of us have unfinished business."

"Fine by me," Flynn said. Reluctantly, he took his hand off the butt of the LeMat revolver.

"We'll tether the horses here and go into the woods after her," Blaine said.

"Are you sure? Maybe we should just wait here. She'll come out sooner or later. There's only one road back to Washington."

Flynn would have liked to unholster his revolver and shoot Blaine, but short of that, he planned to do what he could to help Miss Carroll escape. It was true what he had said about the road being the only way back to Washington. But if they waited for her to come back out, it would soon be dark enough that they might not see her and she could escape.

But Blaine was having none of that. "I said we are going into the woods after her. That's an order. You do still take orders, don't you, Lieutenant?"

"Yes, sir."

Quickly, they secured the horses. Considering the number of fleeing soldiers in the area, Flynn hoped that the horses would still be there when they got back. He would hate to lose the bay roan.

Blaine led the way into the woods. Blackberry thorns clawed at them, but their heavy wool uniforms were more resistant than Miss Carroll's dress had been. It was easy to follow her trail, considering that she had left several strips from her dress in her wake. Nonetheless, the thorns scratched at their hands and faces. Both men cursed.

The blackberry thicket ended where the woods began, the heavy trunks of oaks and hickories marching away into the shadows.

"She could be anywhere!" Flynn shouted into the stillness.

"Be quiet, you fool. She'll hear you."

That was the idea, Flynn thought. He hoped that Miss Carroll had the good sense to run in the other direction.

Blaine had taken out his pistol and was pointing it toward the murky woods ahead.

"We're supposed to capture her, not shoot her," Flynn pointed out. His hand drifted toward his pistol, his eyes on Blaine's gun. If Captain Blaine decided to shoot him now, nobody would be the wiser.

"I'm not taking any chances with that woman," Blaine said. "If she doesn't surrender, I'll shoot her."

Blaine moved deeper into the woods. The sun was still up, though low on the horizon, but among the trees, it was as if dusk had already arrived. The cool shade provided a welcome relief from the July heat. If Blaine hadn't been there, the woods might even have been pleasant.

They reached a tiny brook that ran among moss-covered boulders. The cool, clear water proved irresistible. Flynn got down on his belly and drank deeply where the water had pooled. Beside him, he became aware of a footprint in the soft, damp earth. It was slowly filling with water, showing that it was freshly made.

Captain Blaine saw it, too. "She went this way!" he muttered, heading downstream.

"Are you sure? Maybe she went deeper into the woods."

But the captain was already following the brook. Flynn had no choice but to follow.

They spotted another footprint. And another. Blaine began to hurry, losing his footing once or twice on the slippery stones. His knee-high, stylish boots were made for riding, not hunting through the woods. Flynn wore more practical boots that were battered and dusty.

Flynn had to give the Carroll woman credit. She had managed to outrun Blaine so far. Considering that she was also a spy and a writer, she was a woman of many talents.

But her luck was running out. Up ahead, a shadowy figure moved ghost-like through the trees lining the brook.

"You there, stop!" Blaine shouted. "Stop, damn you!"

Miss Carroll did not obey, but ran even faster downstream. Blaine started running after her, but slipped again on the slick stones and almost fell, reaching out for a tree branch to catch himself.

"Damn that woman," he muttered, then raised his revolver and sighted coldly along the barrel.

Flynn realized that the captain was unlikely to miss at this distance, and that he definitely wasn't intending to shoot over Miss Carroll's head.

He swatted Blaine's arm and the gun fired harmlessly into the air. The sharp sound was like a thunderclap of sin in the cathedral of the quiet woods.

"What the devil are you doing?" Blaine demanded. He waved the pistol in Flynn's direction. For a moment, Flynn feared that the captain would shoot him, after all.

"Colonel Devere wants her alive."

"Then you had better catch her yourself if you don't want me to shoot her," Blaine said. "I'm no damn good in these boots."

Flynn nodded and started after her, leaving Blaine to follow as best he could. He could see that the gentle brook flowed toward the edge of the woods and the road beyond that led to a bridge, which meant that this must be Cub Run, a tributary of Bull Run.

He tried his best not to overtake her, but up ahead, Miss Carroll slipped on the rocks and fell heavily. He glanced over his shoulder. Blaine was now some distance behind him.

"Run for the road!" he called out as loudly as he dared, hoping that Blaine couldn't hear him. "It's your best chance to get back to Washington City."

It was hard to know if Miss Carroll had heard him or not, but she picked herself up and ran for the daylight at the edge of the woods.

Flynn glanced over his shoulder and shouted to Blaine, "Captain, you'd better hurry. She's getting away!"

Blaine cursed and raised his pistol. Flynn ducked behind a tree, half expecting the shot to be aimed at him. But Captain Blaine was shooting at Miss Carroll. He fired again. Then she pushed her way out of the woods and was gone from sight.

Blaine had caught up. "Hurry! Don't just stand there, you Irish fool! You're letting her get away."

Flynn gritted his teeth. Why was he putting up with this man? Because if he returned to Devere's Legion without Blaine, the colonel would be suspicious, knowing their history. And right now, Devere's Legion was the only safe berth that he had—and his only hope of making sure that Jay was all right. Besides, Flynn never had been one for shooting a man in the back.

Muttering a curse, he followed Blaine out of the woods, back out into the open. Once again, they had to fight their way through a screen of prickly blackberries and multi-flora rose.

Up ahead, they caught a glimpse of Miss Carroll joining the stream of people on the road toward the Cub Run bridge just ahead. Flynn could see that once the gentle brook left the woods, that it widened quickly and the banks grew steep. The bridge was the best way across, but it was creating a bottleneck for the mass of retreating soldiers and civilians.

"Let's get the horses," Captain Blaine said. "We know where she's headed. She won't get far on foot."

They had to backtrack along the edge of the woods in order to get back to where they had left their horses. Flynn breathed a sigh of relief when he saw that the horse was still there, along with Blaine's horse, both animals happily munching at some foliage.

But maybe not for long. A pair of Union soldiers had spotted the horses and were hurrying toward them. Considering that they were closer, they were going to get there first. After trying to flee the battle-field on foot, they must have thought that the appearance of two rider-less horses was a godsend.

Beside Flynn, the captain's pistol cracked again. He had fired a shot at the Union soldiers. Only one of them still carried a musket—many of the retreating soldiers had lost theirs, or thrown them away. He raised the musket, which would be far more accurate than a pistol at this distance. There was a puff and smoke as he fired. The ball whistled over Flynn's head.

"Damn you!" Flynn shouted, firing off a shot with the LeMat. The soldier dropped his musket and cried out as the bullet grazed his shoulder. Both soldiers turned and ran.

They reached the horses and mounted, then dashed toward the road. A flood of retreating soldiers moved toward the relative safety on the other side of the bridge. However, what had begun as an orderly retreat was now a chaotic rush away from an enemy army that must surely be giving chase.

They were no longer organized units, but only small groups of soldiers who had eaten and fought together. As Flynn had told his own cavalrymen yesterday, the only men who mattered on the battlefield were the ones that you fought beside. These men had stuck together as the rest of the Union units fell apart.

Some soldiers were wounded, wrapped in bloody bandages, and they limped along with the help of friends. Muskets had been turned into crutches. As with the soldiers who had tried to take their horses, many of the defeated troops had discarded their arms. A musket and ammunition were too much to carry.

Although Flynn and Blaine wore Confederate uniforms, scarcely anyone paid them any attention. After all, the troops on the road wore a confusing array of uniforms in these early days of the war. A few even wore gray, which was a popular uniform color for soldiers from local and state militias. Some of these uniforms featured so much gold or silver braid that a private could be mistaken for a general.

Carriages carrying whole families were added to the mix, along with civilians on foot. Joining in the picnic atmosphere that had preceded the fight, they had come out to see the battle. In the end, they had gotten more than they bargained for. Having come out to witness a battle out of curiosity, they now found themselves caught up in the bloody aftermath.

Aside from woods and fields, the only landmark in sight was a farmhouse and a white canvas hospital tent that had been erected in the distance. He could see crowds of wounded Union soldiers lying or sitting in the grass around it, awaiting treatment. An ambulance trundled away, apparently beginning its journey carrying some of those wounded back to Washington. It would be an arduous trip over more than twenty miles of rough road in the back of a wagon.

On horseback, Flynn and Blaine had a clear view of it all. Behind them, Flynn could see much of the same—a sea of retreating soldiers. So far, no pursuing Confederates had come into sight. Around him, Flynn had heard a few warnings shouted about the Dark Horse Cavalry being on the way. It seemed that after their brutal charge earlier today on the battlefield that Devere's Legion had gained a fierce reputation.

"Do you see her?" Blaine demanded.

"No," Flynn replied, although he wouldn't have told Blaine if he did. With any luck, Miss Carroll would lose herself in the crowd.

But she had no such luck. Blaine stood in his stirrups, then pointed. "There she is! After her!"

Flynn looked where Blaine had pointed. Sure enough, he caught a glimpse of a female head and shoulders among the soldiers.

Blaine was already surging toward her, trying to force his horse through the crowd on the road. But it was not that easy. Men cursed at him as the horse shoved at them. A wounded man, hobbling on two bloody legs, toppled into the dusty road and was nearly trampled. If the soldiers hadn't noticed the Confederate uniforms before, they certainly did now.

"Look at him, boys! He's a Confederate! Grab him!"

One or two soldiers reached for Blaine's legs, trying to pull him from the saddle, but he managed to rush ahead and they lost their grip. Blaine neatly maneuvered the horse away from more grasping hands. Even Flynn had to grudgingly admit that the man was an excellent horseman.

Flynn was trying to follow, but a knot of men stubbornly pulling a field gun had gotten in his way. They seemed determined not to let the field gun fall into enemy hands. With the slow-moving cannon in his way, there was no going forward. He tried to ride around them, but found his path blocked by a carriage. Meanwhile, he could see that Blaine had found a gap in the crowd and was spurring forward.

Frustrated, Flynn tried to get his horse to push its way through, but the bay roan was too gentle.

"Where do you think you're goin', Johnny Reb?" someone shouted.

Now that Blaine had pushed ahead, it was Flynn who was attracting unwanted attention. On horseback, and wearing a gray uniform, he stood out and made an easy target for the irate, defeated Union soldiers.

"You don't understand," he said. "I'm trying to help that woman up there!"

"Drag him off that horse!" someone shouted.

A big soldier grabbed at Flynn's left arm, trying to get hold of the reins. Flynn hammered his right fist into the man's face and he fell away.

But the sight of the soldier with a bloody nose only enraged the crowd. More hands reached for him and the horse whinnied in fright. In some ways, it was much like the mob in Baltimore had been that day in April when he had first run into young Jay Warfield. A mob had a mind of its own and there was no reasoning with it. You might as well try and reason with a rattlesnake.

"Damn you all!" Flynn shouted, then forced the horse off the road and into the field. Two or three soldiers started to follow, but saw Flynn put his hand to his revolver and they thought better of it. They turned around and joined the flow of retreating troops and civilians. No one seemed to give the gray-coated rider a second thought.

Here on a battlefield with thousands of men within musket range, Flynn found himself utterly alone and more than a little lost.

CHAPTER TWENTY-TWO

FLYNN HAD ESCAPED FROM THE ANGRY TROOPS—AT LEAST FOR NOW. But Captain Blaine was still on the road, intent on riding after Anna Ella Carroll. Flynn had no hope of catching up to them—not unless he wanted to fight his way through the throng of hostile Union troops. Reluctantly, he turned his horse away from the road, wondering what to do next.

Maybe it was a bit late considering the circumstances, but Flynn had to wonder why he should concern himself anymore with Miss Carroll. He'd been ready to be done with her and thought that he'd seen the last of her in Richmond. Encountering her on the battlefield had changed the situation all over again. Part of it was that Rose Greenhow had paid him well to see her back to safety, with more money to come upon her return to Washington, and he felt compelled to do what he could to uphold his end of the bargain. Flynn might be many things, but he was also a man of his word.

But that wasn't the only reason. In part, he disliked Captain Blaine so much that he would do whatever he could to thwart the man from carrying out Colonel Devere's orders.

More than that, Flynn realized that he admired the woman. She was smart, contrary, independent. She might be headstrong and foolish, bordering on arrogant, but there was nothing vain about her actions. Everything that she did was for the Union, a cause that she believed in strongly. Being Irish, Flynn knew a thing or two about fool-hardy patriots, whose hearts were often bigger than their heads. They ignored the odds against them. He thought that Miss Carroll was cut from the same cloth.

Seeing that he was much closer now to the hospital tent, he decided to ride in that direction. The heat and the hard ride had given him a brutal thirst. The drink from the brook back in the woods had curbed that only temporarily and his canteen was empty. Maybe he could get a drink at that tent. It was likely that his gray uniform might cause less of a stir there than on the road.

He entered the hospital yard and began to see the wreckage of war up close. Men were strewn wherever the stretcher-bearers had left them. Some sat up and smoked or talked. Others lay so listlessly that they didn't have the energy to brush away the flies that had settled on their faces. A few stared sightlessly at the Virginia sky, help for them having come too late. A pair of black men worked carrying away the dead.

Flynn felt compassion for those wounded men. They had started the day heroically, marching off to war in high hopes. Now, they were returning broken and bloody in defeat. He had no hatred of Union soldiers. He didn't give a damn about the politics of either side. If it hadn't been for the fact that he had agreed to be Rose Greenhow's errand boy, he might just as easily be wearing a blue uniform.

Mixed with the wounded Union soldiers were several injured Confederates. What if Jay was among them? He could only hope that if Jay had been wounded that he had been brought here or another field hospital, and that he wasn't laying out in the open with night coming on. Jay's being wounded, captured—or worse—seemed to be the only explanation for why he had not rejoined the legion after the cavalry charge. For better or worse, he felt responsible for the lad's fate.

He tied the roan and picked his way among the wounded—there were so many. He was pleased to see that a few women and boys were taking water to the wounded and they seemed to be giving the rebels equal treatment. However, he did not see Jay anywhere. He didn't know if he should be relieved or even more worried.

Giving up his search of the field, he entered the massive hospital tent, pushing through the canvas flaps. The heat inside was incredible with the July sun beating down, but the flaps and sides had been left down in a vain attempt to keep out the flies that landed everywhere, tormenting the wounded.

Even worse than the heat was the smell. It was a nauseating mixture of blood, offal, sweat, and a chemical whiff of the ether being used to knock out patients before they went under the saw.

Then there were the sounds. Agonized cries, of course, and young men calling for their mothers. Maybe it was only Flynn's imagination, but above it all, he seemed to hear the relentless wet rasping of the surgeons' saws against flesh and bone. The noise sent a shiver up his spine and he felt slightly sick to his stomach. The worst of the screams emanated from the tables where the surgeons worked. There seemed to be a lack of ether or it wasn't effective in all cases. Some men were simply given a stick to bite down on.

Wherever a Minié ball or piece of shrapnel had mangled an arm or a leg, the only hope of preventing death by gangrene was to saw off the limb. The surgeons were doing this as rapidly as possible. As soon as one man was carried off the table, another one took his place. Flynn couldn't know it, but this was only the first such day of many to come. More than 60,000 soldiers would lose an arm or leg in the war.

As a boy, Flynn had survived the trip to America in the stinking hold of a famine ship, with all of its accompanying misery, but this was much worse. The smell alone made him dizzy and Flynn staggered.

"Steady there," an officer said, catching him by the elbow. Judging by the bloody apron the man wore, he must be one of the surgeons. The sheer weight of Flynn sagging against him threw the smaller man off balance. "Are you hurt?"

"No, sir," Flynn said, regaining his balance. "By the grace of God I am not. I am looking for a friend."

Flynn was still wearing his gray coat with its painted-on officer's insignia, although it was now flecked liberally with mud and blood, and a bullet hole or two had been added to the ones that the moths had made.

A soldier who seemed to be the officer's orderly caught sight of Flynn's uniform and his eyes widened. "Captain Caldwell, look out! Can't you see that this man is a rebel?"

"There are no enemies in this tent," Caldwell snapped at the orderly. The officer smelled strongly of liquor. Given the hell that he worked in, who could blame him for drinking? The officer turned his attention back to Flynn. "Can you tell me anything about your friend? Maybe I have seen him."

"He is a young man, not much more than a boy, really. Sandy hair, blue eyes, comes up to about my shoulder. He'll be wearing a Confederate uniform."

"Relative?"

"No, just a lad that I seem to keep getting out of one fix after another. In fact, he signed up to fight to spite his brother, if you can believe it." Flynn sighed, suddenly exhausted, and nearly overcome by the misery around him. It didn't help that Jay was missing and he'd lost sight of Miss Carroll on the road. He shook his head woefully. He was wondering why he was telling all this to the surgeon, but Caldwell nodded as he listened. "I've lost track of him, along with a woman I was supposed to protect. I'm not much of a soldier, am I?"

The officer said, "Go look for your friend. I've grouped the Confederates over in that corner."

Flynn nodded his gratitude at the officer and headed in that direction. He passed between the rows of broken men. Uniforms that had once been bright with colorful trim were now stained with blood. This tent was the last place that he wanted to be. The awful sights were a good reminder that Flynn did not care much for the so-called glory of war. He did not put much stock in politicians. He thought oaths were only so many pretty words. Honor meant nothing to him; it was a luxury for rich men. He did not care about patriotism and he did not suppose that a man whose guts were leaking from his belly cared much about it, either. He saw all these sights and more. It was a nightmarish place. At each step, his brain urged him to duck out through the tent flaps into the fresh air. But in hopes of finding his young friend, he would gladly search through hell itself.

Lying in the corner of the tent, he spotted a young soldier around Jay's age. Was it Jay? He hurried over, but saw at once that it was not Jay.

The young soldier's head was bandaged, but that wasn't the worst of his wounds. His right leg was missing below the knee. He'd already had his turn at one of the operating tables.

The young soldier opened his eyes and looked up at him with curiosity. "Who are you, sir?"

"Just a soldier looking for a friend, and I thought for a moment that I'd found him. How are you, lad?" Flynn asked.

"I'll live," the young soldier said. "That's more than can be said for some. Sir, would it be too much trouble to ask you for a drink of water?"

"Not at all," Flynn said. He helped the young soldier sit upright enough that he could drink from a tin cup of water that had been placed near his cot. The heat inside the tent was nearly unbearable. He found it so stifling that it was hard to breathe, but the youth did not complain. Flynn hoped for the sake of the wounded that it would cool down after sunset.

"Thank you."

Flynn nodded and moved on. He saw row after row of wounded men, most of whom lay on blankets on the grass. It soon became clear that Jay was not among the Confederate wounded. He didn't know whether to be relieved or disappointed. He still wasn't sure of Jay's fate. Reluctantly, he started back toward the entrance of the tent.

"Did you find your friend among the wounded?" asked the physician, who was preparing to get back to work. He had rinsed his hands in a bowl of pink-tinged water and was wiping them on a blood-stained towel.

"No." Flynn looked around. "How do you stand it, sir? Seeing these wounded is almost more than I can bear. When people are waving their flags back home, they don't think about the hospital tent, do they?"

" 'Few die well that die in battle,' " Caldwell muttered.

"That sounds like Shakespeare."

"It is. Maybe it's a good thing that your young friend isn't here. Go find him. While you're at it, go find that woman you mentioned and do right by her. A woman shouldn't be left alone among all these men, especially with night coming on. Not all of them are as honorable as we would like to think."

"I wouldn't even know where to begin to look for them."

"Look at these wounded men around you who are helpless. You still have two good feet and two good hands, so what are you complaining about?"

"I'm not complaining."

"Good. Now go and find your friends."

CHAPTER TWENTY-THREE

FLYNN LEFT THE TENT, FEELING NEWLY ENERGIZED BY THE CHANCE encounter with the Union surgeon. Although the surgeon had appeared well on his way to being intoxicated, he had spoken some words of wisdom. Flynn had no choice but to do what he could to help Miss Carroll. Perhaps in the process, he would find Jay.

He retrieved his horse and took a slug of whiskey from the bottle in his saddlebag. A group of wounded men sat on the grass nearby, eyeing the bottle greedily. "Can you spare a drink?" one of them asked.

Flynn tossed him the bottle. "Keep it," he said.

He rode toward the turnpike. Instead of joining the throng on the road, however, he struck out cross country, riding directly toward the Cub Run bridge. The bridge had created a bottleneck due to the sheer number of military wagons, ambulances, and civilian carriages that were trying to use the narrow crossing. Traffic on the road had slowed and spilled out into the fields. Soldiers on foot were sliding down the steep creek banks and then struggling up the other side. He was sure that the congestion at the bridge would be his best chance of finding Miss Carroll.

As Flynn approached, he could see that a wagon had overturned near the bridge. Soldiers struggled to calm the team of horses tangled into the harness while trying to upright the wagon. Meanwhile, the road leading to the bridge grew even more crowded.

The crowd was beginning to panic, worried that they would be caught up by the Confederate advance.

"The Dark Horse Cavalry is coming!" someone shouted, upon seeing Flynn approach. "They'll cut us down!"

The anxious shouts died when they saw that Flynn was alone, but their fears of enemy cavalry sweeping down upon the road were not unfounded. Flynn thought it was just the thing that Colonel Devere might be mad enough to do.

It didn't help matters that a battery of Confederate artillery was now firing randomly in the direction of the bridge, harassing the retreating Unions troops. Shells burst in the trees beside the road, and the occasional solid shot *karoomed* overhead. They'd better get that mess cleared up soon and get the road open or there's going to be hell to pay, he thought.

Flynn dismounted and joined the men trying to right the over-turned wagon. It seemed to be the best way to get the traffic flowing again.

"Grab that corner and lift!" he shouted. "Put your back into it."

A Union soldier joined him. Working shoulder to shoulder, the two men heaved and pushed. It wasn't helping that the crowd pressed at them from every side, eager to get past them, but leaving them no space to maneuver.

"Give them room!" a woman shouted with authority, her voice cracking like a whip.

The voice was familiar. Flynn was surprised to see that it was Miss Carroll who was doing the shouting. She stood beside a tall, older man in a long linen duster. Like Miss Carroll, the man had stretched out his arms to hold back the crowd in an effort to give Flynn and the other men enough space to work.

"Push!" Flynn shouted.

At first, the weight of the wagon seemed unwilling to budge, but the broad-shouldered man in the duster joined in, and suddenly the corner of the wagon began to inch upward. With one last heave, the men sent the wagon crashing back onto all four wheels. The wagon rocked back and forth, threatening to tip over in the opposite direction, then settled upright.

With the wagon out of the way, it looked as if the traffic was finally going to get moving again. Flynn turned to say something to Miss Carroll, but suddenly found himself flying through the air. His ears rang, but he could still hear people screaming, and the terrified whinnying of horses. Stunned, it took him a moment to realize what had happened. A shell had made a direct hit on the bridge.

He looked up to see Miss Carroll standing over him. "Well, don't just lie there, Lieutenant Flynn," she scolded. "Get up!"

The man in the duster helped him to his feet. "Are you hurt?"

Flynn shook his head to clear it, feeling as if he'd just taken a roundhouse punch to the head. "I'll be all right."

Realization seemed to dawn on the man. He shifted his grip on a shotgun that he carried, looking like a man who knew how to use it. "Why, you're a Confederate officer, aren't you!"

Miss Carroll stepped between them. "It's all right, Congressman," she said. "I know this man. He can be trusted."

Flynn looked the man up and down in surprise. "Congressman?"

"This is Congressman Ely of New York," Miss Carroll explained. "But now is not the time to discuss politics or even for proper introductions, gentlemen. I suggest we make haste back to Washington."

"Along with the whole damn Union army, it looks like," Congressman Ely said. "Lincoln will have McDowell's head on a platter for this defeat. It's a debacle, I tell you."

Another shell burst nearby. "We need to get across this bridge!" Miss Carroll said. "What if the Confederates attack?"

Her words of warning suddenly seemed to have come too late. Frightened shouts rang out from the road behind them and Flynn heard hoofbeats in the field beyond.

"It's the Dark Horse Cavalry!" someone shouted again. "We're under attack!"

Fear spread through the crowd. Instead of taking up defensive positions against an attack, many of the defeated Union soldiers flew into a panic instead. They slid down the bank and splashed their way across the shallow creek, pushing and shoving one another out of the way.

Some were caught in the stampede and nearly drowned in water that wasn't more than two feet deep.

But once again, it was a false alarm. Instead of an entire legion of Confederate cavalry, it was just one man on horseback, riding through the field. He wore a bright red plume in his hat. And he was riding hellbent for leather.

The figure was instantly familiar. None other than Captain Blaine was riding toward them at a gallop. Flynn had found Miss Carroll, but he didn't seem to have lost Blaine.

Like Flynn had earlier, Blaine must have gotten sidetracked by the press of the crowd, but no longer. Blaine reached the road, scattering men in his path. It was either clear out of the way, or be run down. His surefooted horse managed not to trample anyone. Blaine rode directly toward the bridge, his eyes on his quarry.

"There you are!" he shouted.

Miss Carroll sighed. "I managed to lose him back there in the crowd. I hoped that I had seen the last of that wretched man."

"You know this man as well?" The congressman seemed amused. "I must say that you lead an exciting life, Miss Carroll."

As Blaine rode up, he spotted Flynn and his eyes widened in surprise. "Where did *you* come from?"

"I was in that hospital tent back there, looking for Jay Warfield. I didn't find him."

"Never mind that. The young fool is probably dead. Now that you're here, help me get her on the horse so we can take her back to Colonel Devere."

Blaine vaulted lightly down from the horse, graceful as always, and took a step toward Miss Carroll.

Both Flynn and Congressman Ely blocked his path. The congressman was holding his shotgun balanced in the crook of his elbow.

"Miss Carroll, do you wish to go with this man?" he asked.

"No, I do not."

Blaine looked from the congressman to Flynn. "What are you doing?" he asked Flynn.

"She's not going with you," Flynn said. "She's going back to Washington."

Blaine reached for his revolver, but Flynn grabbed his hand and after a brief struggle, managed to twist the weapon from his grip. Flynn tossed the revolver into the creek below.

But Blaine would not be thwarted. Cursing, he took a step back and drew his sword.

Flynn drew his own saber.

The congressman had leveled his shotgun at Blaine. "Do you want me to shoot him?"

"Not yet," Flynn said. "Only if I start to lose."

The two men circled one another, swords raised. Instinctively, the crowd made room for them, although some pushed past, desperate to get across the bridge.

It was the duel, all over again.

Another artillery shell burst overhead, making everyone flinch and duck. The Confederate battery was still at work. A solid shot passed overhead with a telltale *whoosh*.

Quick as a panther, Blaine made a sweeping attack with his sword. Flynn parried and struck back, but the point of his blade cut into the empty space that Blaine had occupied a moment before.

Flynn cursed under his breath. He was no swordsman. His strategy consisted of trying to hammer past the captain's blade. If this duel went on for any length of time, he didn't like his chances.

Blaine slashed savagely into the opening that Flynn had left him. It might have been a killing blow against a weaker man, but Flynn blocked the blade with a grip of iron. The shock of the blades colliding forced Blaine off balance and he lost his hold on the sword, which clattered to the wooden floor of the bridge.

Flynn lunged, intending to skewer Blaine on the sword point. Behind him, he heard Miss Carroll gasp as she realized what was about to happen next.

But Blaine was too quick. He danced out of the way and as Flynn's arm went past, he gave him a tremendous shove. Flynn fell sideways, just barely managing to keep his feet.

He spun, blade at the ready. To his surprise, Blaine was standing just out of reach, pointing at Flynn's face with a small pistol that he had retrieved from his uniform coat.

Flynn froze. "Why Captain Blaine, I wouldn't have expected you to use dirty tricks like that."

"A gentleman would have let me retrieve my sword," Blaine said. "This derringer will be good enough to finish off an Irish dog like you."

"Do you want me to shoot him now?" the congressman asked.

"Just get Miss Carroll out of here," Flynn growled.

"I always wondered whose side you were on, Flynn," the captain said. "It seems clear that Miss Carroll was not the only spy. It's just a shame that I won't be able to hang you properly."

Flynn saw Blaine begin to squeeze the trigger.

"Damn you to hell, Blaine," Flynn said.

Before he could fire, Flynn felt a hot rush of air pass him by. *Whoosh.* A split second later, Captain Blaine was gone.

One moment, Captain Blaine had been standing there about to shoot him, and the next, he was a blur, flying through the air like a leaf caught in a sudden gust of wind.

It had all happened so fast. A little stunned, Flynn began to piece together what had taken place. A round of solid shot had struck Captain Blaine, knocking him into the creek below. Flynn peered over the railing at what remained of the cavalry officer, bobbing in the water. The body was an unrecognizable lump of raw meat and torn uniform. Just beneath the surface of the muddy creek, a bit of gold braid gleamed in the last of the sunlight. A waterlogged red ostrich plume floated nearby.

"Dear God," said the congressman, who had joined him at the rail. He and Miss Carroll had not gotten far. "That's somewhat better than I could have done with my shotgun."

"I suppose he's dead?" asked Miss Carroll, who had not come to the rail.

"Yes."

"Then let us get to Washington," she said. "I still have important information to deliver that could help prevent future debacles like this battle."

"That's an excellent idea," said the congressman. "If I'm not mistaken, that's Senator Carter's carriage on the other side of the bridge. Let me see if he will carry us to Washington."

Miss Carroll turned to Flynn. "Are you coming with us, Lieutenant Flynn?"

"Not yet. I need to see if I can find Jay."

"Very well. I hope that you find him safe and sound." In the distance, the congressman had caught up to the carriage and was calling for her to join him. She started to turn away, then hesitated. "I was wrong about you, Lieutenant Flynn. I always think I know what to expect of people, and yet they manage to prove me wrong. You weren't doing this just for Rose Greenhow's money."

"I wasn't?"

She gave one of her rare smiles. "Perhaps I shall see you soon in Washington, Lieutenant Flynn."

She hurried off to climb into the waiting carriage. The congressman had climbed up onto the seat beside the driver, his shotgun balanced across his knees. Flynn decided that she would be in good hands for the remainder of the journey. Someone had already seized Captain Blaine's horse and galloped away, but to Flynn's surprise, his horse was still tied by the side of the turnpike. He retrieved his horse and rode back toward the Confederate lines.

CHAPTER TWENTY-FOUR

FLYNN RODE AWAY FROM THE TURMOIL AT THE BRIDGE, HEADING back toward the Confederate lines. In many ways, it was like swimming against the current as panicked Union troops and fleeing civilians swarmed up the Warrenton Turnpike, headed in the direction of Alexandria and Washington City, desperate to escape the battlefield and the threat of Confederate pursuit. A day that had come so close to a stunning Union victory, perhaps one that could have settled the war, had ended in utter defeat and chaos.

Some of the fleeing troops and civilians wondered if the Union capital itself would be safe. With its army in disarray, there was little to stop Confederate troops from capturing the city. What the retreating troops didn't know was that while the Confederate army might have won the field, it was still too disorganized to press its advantage by marching on Washington.

Flynn rode on against the tide, deciding to leave worrying about those matters of strategy to the generals. Despite the fact that Flynn wore a gray uniform, no one paid him any attention beyond a few curious glances. Again, it helped that there was a confusing array of uniforms. Maybe they were just caught off guard by the sight of a lone

Confederate officer riding through the crowd in the opposite direction.

That was just fine by Flynn. He'd had enough fighting for one day. He was glad that the long summer day, which had started well before sunup, was finally coming to an end. The afternoon had long since faded toward evening, although the sun still hung above the trees on the nearby hilltops like a child that didn't want to go to bed. The heat had not relented and he reached for his canteen to take a long drink of lukewarm water. He tilted back the canteen and drank it dry.

As much as he would have liked to join Miss Carroll and her congressman friend for the return trip to the Union capital, leaving the Confederacy behind for good, he had decided to stay. He still hoped to find Jay somewhere on this chaotic battlefield.

He hadn't seen Jay in the hospital tent. His next best chance was back at the legion. If was still alive, it was just possible that Jay had found his way back to the unit.

Flynn's decision to return to the legion wasn't without risks. First and foremost, he wondered what Colonel Devere's reaction would be when Flynn reappeared without Captain Blaine—or Anna Ella Carroll. The colonel had a hot temper. It was unlikely that Flynn would be welcomed with open arms.

But Flynn had made up his mind. He rode on and reached the battlefield itself with all its scenes of destruction: dead horses lay alongside the corpses of men in gray and blue. A few stretcher-bearers moved among the bodies, looking for those who might still be alive. Soldiers searched for missing comrades among the fallen. The butcher's bill had been heavy on both sides. Flynn guessed that there were hundreds of dead, if not thousands. It was true that he had fought in Italy, but the carnage here far overshadowed the Battle of Castelfidardo.

There were overturned caissons and wagons, along with a few Union artillery pieces abandoned because their wheels were smashed to kindling. After so much musket fire and the booming of guns throughout the day, the battlefield sounded eerily hushed as the shadows lengthened toward evening. Flynn was not especially superstitious, but he hoped to be well away from the battlefield before night-fall. He didn't expect the spirits of the dead to lie easy.

He came across a ragged line of Confederate soldiers, standing with fixed bayonets, as if prepared for a Union incursion. They eyed Flynn warily as he approached.

"I'm looking for Devere's Legion," Flynn announced.

The nearest soldier lowered his bayonet. "We thought you must be a Yankee, coming from that direction," the man said. "Can't hardly tell who's who from the uniforms."

Flynn barked a laugh. "If you want to see a Yankee, lad, you'd better hurry back the way I've just come. They're all running for Washington."

His comment pleased the soldiers. "I told you, we could lick them, boys!" one man shouted. He whooped. "We done won the war in one day."

"I sure hope so," Flynn said. "Now, what about the legion?"

"You mean the Dark Horse Cavalry?" the soldier asked. When Flynn nodded, the man waved vaguely behind him. "I reckon they're somewhere back there, sir."

Flynn nodded his thanks to the soldier and rode on. He could tell that the bay roan was tired because once or twice the horse stumbled over debris in the field.

"Easy now," he said to the horse, giving him a reassuring pat. "It's not much farther."

He realized that he felt equally exhausted. It had been a long day filled with fighting and grisly sights. While he did not regret the fact that Captain Blaine was dead, the man had been killed brutally, turned inside out by a round of solid shot. Flynn would not forget the image of that mangled and bloody body floating face down in the muddy waters of Cub Run anytime soon. He shook his head to clear it.

He had promised his horse that they didn't have far to go. Fortunately, he wasn't proven wrong. He soon spotted a couple of familiar faces on horseback.

They saw him as well and waved. "Lieutenant Flynn," shouted one of the men, and he realized it was Devere's adjutant. "We thought we had lost you, sir."

"I thought that I'd been lost myself. What a day it has been."

The adjutant looked him up and down and then asked the obvious question. "What about Captain Blaine? I saw you both ride off after that spy."

"I'm afraid that Captain Blaine didn't make it."

"What happened?"

"He was cut down by one of our own artillery shells back on the bridge."

The adjutant nodded, but gave a doubtful expression. Everyone in the legion knew about the bad blood between Flynn and Captain Blaine. The two men had fought a duel, after all. Given their history, it wasn't surprising that two men had ridden out, but that only one had returned. "Colonel Devere has been asking for you," the adjutant said. "He gave orders that you should report to him immediately—if and when you returned to camp."

Flynn said, "Aye, I will go see the colonel, although I'm sure he will be disappointed that it's me who's returning, and not his lackey. But tell me, have you seen young Jay Warfield?"

The adjutant shook his head. "I haven't seen him since the charge this morning. He wouldn't be the only man that we've lost this day, sad to say. Now, if I were you, I would go find the colonel straight away."

Flynn rode on, looking for the colonel's headquarters. It wasn't hard to find. Devere had once again had his tent set up in the field, complete with the legion's pennant flying from the topmost peak, as if he was some knight of yore on the fields of Agincourt.

Reluctantly, Flynn approached the tent. He did not expect a warm reception from the colonel. But he was under orders—he had no choice but to report to the commanding officer. He knew that Devere would be as calm and rational as your typical Southern gentleman—which was to say, not at all.

After nodding to the guard, Flynn brushed aside the flap and ducked low to enter the tent. Devere sat at a camp table, working by candlelight in the dusky interior. He was bare-headed, pomade gleaming in his sandy hair that was flecked with gray at the temples. A pair of reading glasses that Flynn hadn't seen before was perched on the end of his nose. Devere snatched them off as Flynn entered the tent.

"Lieutenant Flynn," Devere said flatly, remaining seated behind the desk.

Flynn drew his tired body to some semblance of attention. Flynn couldn't help but notice that Devere kept a revolver within reach on his desk, apparently using it as a paperweight.

Flynn heard a noise behind him and turned to see Sergeant Creighton entering the tent after him. Silently, he went and stood in one corner of the tent, looking like the watchdog that he was.

It was hard to know if Devere was disappointed at Flynn's return, or by the fact that Flynn was alone. "Where is Captain Blaine?"

"I'm afraid that he was killed, sir. We were at the Cub Run bridge, trying to capture Miss Carroll, when one of our own artillery rounds struck him dead."

Pointedly, Flynn left out the part where he and Blaine had fought at the bridge. He hoped that Devere would never learn the truth because there would be hell to pay. It was even possible that if Devere couldn't hang one spy, then he would make do with another.

Slowly, Devere reacted to the news of Captain Blaine's death. Flynn had never been sure whether Devere had actually been fond of the captain, but the man had served him well as his second in command of the legion. He seemed to run through a range of emotions. Sorrow was not one of them. His eyebrows arched in surprise, but then his expression hardened into a glare.

"That will be all, Sergeant," Devere said, dismissing Creighton from the tent.

On his way out, Creighton gave Flynn a nasty grin with his tobacco-stained teeth that seemed to mean, *this isn't over yet.*

Once they were alone again, the colonel fixed his glare on Flynn and said, "If I thought for a moment that you were responsible in any way for Captain Blaine's death, I'd have you strung up from the nearest tree."

"Sir, it was a terrible thing. We were both on the bridge trying to stop Miss Carroll. You were right about that woman, sir. She had taken up with a United States congressman. He had a shotgun, you see, and he wasn't about to let us seize the woman without a fight. That's when Blaine was hit. It could have been either one of us."

"Thus are the fates of war," Devere said, still not looking entirely convinced. "And what of the spy, Miss Carroll?"

"I have to report that she escaped, sir. The artillery was shelling the bridge and there was a great deal of confusion. She went off with the congressman, who had a carriage waiting."

"They couldn't have gotten far."

"I suspect that by now they are well on the way to Washington," Flynn added hastily, half afraid that Devere might gather the legion ride out after her, fulfilling the retreating Yankees' fears about the Dark Horse Cavalry.

"Very well," he finally said, and turned back to his reports, effectively dismissing Flynn.

But the colonel wasn't done with him, after all. As Flynn turned toward the tent flap, the colonel spoke once more. "I will have my eye on you, Lieutenant."

Gratefully, Flynn parted the tent flaps with a sigh of relief, feeling as if he had escaped yet another battle. If he had worried before that Devere was an enemy, he had no doubts now. He would need to watch out for Devere and Sergeant Creighton, who was the sort of man who would slip a knife into your back for a bottle of whiskey.

Shrugging off the thought, Flynn walked on toward the main camp, leading the bay roan. He nodded at familiar faces that had survived this day and was saddened by the absence of others. Perhaps Bull Run had been a Confederate victory, but at a terrible price.

The one face that he sought more than any other, however, belonged to Jay Warfield.

"Has anyone seen Jay?" he asked one cavalryman after another, but was met with a shake of the head.

Flynn sat by a campfire and accepted a cup of coffee. He would have liked something stronger, but that was not to be had in camp. He almost regretted giving away the last of his whiskey to those wounded troops. He sipped the coffee. It tasted like it had been brewed with rusty nails, but he realized it was the first thing approaching nourishment he'd had other than water for many hours. A handful of sugar had been added to the coffee pot, and he welcomed the sweet taste. He blew on the coffee to cool it and then took a much deeper gulp.

"Save some for me," he heard a familiar voice say.

He looked up, astonished to see young Jay Warfield standing there. The lad had his left arm in a bandage, but otherwise appeared safe and sound.

"You're hurt," Flynn said with concern.

"Grazed by a bullet," Jay said.

"What the hell happened to you today?"

"I rode off after those Yankees and we got cut off," Jay said. "That's when I was wounded. I ended up having to hide in some woods with two other fellows until the Union troops began to retreat and we could get back to our own lines."

"Let me see that arm," Flynn said.

He unwrapped the dirty bandage. The bullet had cut a furrow through the lad's arm, but by some miracle had missed hitting bone. Flynn shuddered, recalling the amputations he had witnessed in the Union field hospital.

Using a canteen of water from Bull Run, he washed the wound until fresh blood flowed.

Jay winced. "What are you doing?"

"The blood will clean it out," Flynn said.

"I never took you for a nurse."

"Oh, I've fixed a hurt or two in my day, but usually on myself." By way of explanation, Flynn touched a scar at the corner of his eye that he'd gotten in a bare-knuckle boxing match. An elderly doctor with shaking hands had offered to sew it up, but Flynn had opted to wield the needle himself.

He did the same now for Jay, sewing the edges of the wound shut. Jay winced as the needle went in and out. "Can't you hurry that up? You're not sewing a quilt."

"Just another stitch or two." Satisfied, he wrapped Jay's wound up tight with a clean bandage. "Keep the dirt out of it and you'll be right as rain soon enough."

"It's just a scratch," Jay insisted, but his pained expression said otherwise.

"A gallant wound," Flynn corrected him. "The young ladies of Richmond will find that quite appealing."

"There's only one young lady I care about, and she's back home in Maryland."

"You really are a fool, aren't you?" Flynn laughed. "What you need is another visit to Maude's place."

Jay reddened at the mention of the bordello, but he didn't offer any argument against it. Maybe he was too tired. He ate some beans and salt pork, then rolled himself into his blanket and slept, following the example of many other exhausted cavalrymen and soldiers.

* * *

IN THE MORNING, the Confederate army began its withdrawal from Manassas. Rather than push its advantage, the bulk of General Beauregard's army was returning to Richmond. While some argued that they should strike at Washington while the iron was still hot, the truth was that his army wasn't prepared to do so. Like Jay, many of the men had minor wounds or were simply exhausted. Food was in short supply, the creeks had been trampled into muddy trickles, and they had expended a great deal of ammunition in the fight. Beauregard might as well have ordered them to march to the moon.

The legion joined the troops making their way through Virginia. Unlike the Union army that had retreated like a dog with his tail between his legs, the gray-clad troops held their heads high. They had been victorious. The weather had turned rainy, but the warm summer rain did little to dampen their spirits. As word of the victory spread, a few people gathered at the crossroads to hail them.

But the real crowd waited in Richmond. Bells rang from every church steeple as the troops returned. Children ran to give flowers to the soldiers and young boys fell into step beside the long gray columns, marching with sticks over their shoulders.

The newspapers were full of accounts of the battle, but one article in particular caused a sensation. It appeared under the name of Anna Ella Carroll and had been reprinted from the *Washington Star*. With the title, *A Letter from Richmond*, the woman had written in detail about the

South's readiness for war in less than flattering terms, including damaging specifics about arms production.

Devere had fumed over the letter, of course. He was not alone. All those who had welcomed Miss Carroll to Richmond as a like-minded Confederate felt betrayed. If she ever returned to the city, there would be fights over who got to tar and feather her.

The letter was quickly forgotten by most in the victory celebrations that filled Richmond. Over the next few days, speeches were made about the valiant troops, politicians thumped their chests, and church services were held for the fallen.

But what the boys wanted was a night on the town, and that was just what Colonel Devere gave them.

Flynn was as eager as anyone for a taste of whiskey. He'd left Jay at a party being given for officers at one of the Richmond mansions—as Flynn had predicted, the lad's bandaged arm attracted the young ladies like moths to a flame. But Flynn did not feel comfortable in the fancy surroundings.

Setting off into the revelry taking place in the city, Flynn had to wonder how long he planned to stay now that he'd seen Jay returned to the legion. He did not plan to remain a soldier for much longer. He planned to desert and make his way to Washington to trade his uniform for civilian clothes again. One battle had been more than enough for him in this war.

He hadn't gone far, however, when he noticed two men following him. They wore civilian clothes at a time when nearly every man in the city was in uniform. This made Flynn uneasy and he remembered how the two thugs had set upon him in Washington. Was this unfinished business concerning the deal that he'd made with Rose Greenhow? Or did this have something to do with Colonel Devere? He wouldn't have put it past Devere to send assassins after him. One way or another, he seemed to have managed to make himself more than a few enemies.

With no interest in taking on the two men, he decided to give them the slip instead. He went around a corner and hid in a dark alley, watching the two men pass by. Satisfied that they had walked on, he emerged from the alley—and found himself face to face with two more men who seemed to have been waiting for him. A carriage had also appeared, as if to block his way. As he sized up the two men, the pair that he had managed to dodge earlier reappeared from around the corner. Flynn was neatly boxed in. Four against one? What was going on?

He had left his revolver behind tonight, but Flynn formed two rock-hard fists. "If it's a fight you want—"

"There will be no need for that," called a voice. Flynn realized that it had come from the carriage. One of the men confronting him turned to open the carriage door and gestured for Flynn to approach.

Keeping an eye on the men, Flynn walked over to the carriage and got in. The springs creaked under Flynn's solid weight. He found himself sitting across from a man wearing an officer's uniform.

"Just who in green glory are you?" Flynn demanded.

"I am Colonel Norris," the officer said.

"Should I have heard of you?"

"I certainly hope not," he said. "I try very hard not to be heard from. However, I have heard of *you*, Mr. Flynn. I believe that we have a mutual friend in Washington City."

Flynn groaned. "I never should have agreed to help that woman. But I'm done with her. I upheld my end of the bargain."

"You mean, by helping a Union spy escape?"

Flynn felt a chill go through him. The man across from him knew more than Flynn might have expected. "You must mean Miss Carroll. That woman was no spy!"

"On the contrary, Mr. Flynn. You read her article in the newspaper, same as I did. Mrs. Greenhow wanted her back from Richmond to prevent her from gathering any more information. Her methods were more gentle than mine would have been, I'm afraid, had I been aware of Miss Carroll's true intent."

"I did what I was asked."

"That's good to know, because I will be asking you to do a lot. The Union has its spies, but so do we. As head of the Confederate Secret Service, I manage those spies."

"Spies? But Colonel, I'm a soldier. An officer in Devere's Legion. Surely you must know that. I can't help you." Flynn wasn't about to tell this man that he planned to desert as soon as he could.

"I'll talk with Devere. From what I understand, he'll be glad to be rid of you." Colonel Norris smiled coldly. "Besides, we both know that you're not really an officer, but just a trumped-up Irishman. From now on, you work for me."

"What do you mean?"

"You'll see. I will be in touch."

Less than a minute later, Flynn found himself standing in the street as the carriage rolled away. But he was not alone. Two of Norris's men had stayed behind, as if to look after him. They stood nearby, arms crossed. He might have taught them a lesson, but he unclenched his fists, suddenly too tired to fight. Once the carriage was out of sight, the two men drifted away.

He had thought that his involvement in the war would soon be over, but he realized that he'd been mistaken.

For Flynn, the war was just beginning.

NOTE TO READERS

Thank you for reading *Rebel Dawn*, which I wrote as a sort of prequel to two other Civil War novels, *Rebel Fever* and *Rebel Train*. Hopefully, more adventures will follow. The story features Tom Flynn, an Irish immigrant who finds himself on the wrong side as the Civil War begins, but makes the best of it. He encounters several characters drawn from real life, especially Anna Ella Carroll, a woman who remains something of an enigma today despite her many talents and her contributions to the Union cause. Devere's Legion itself is loosely based on a company of the 4th Virginia Cavalry, nicknamed the Black Horse Cavalry.

Much of the story is set around the first Battle of Bull Run in July 1861. It's true that the battle had an almost festive air leading up to it, with Washingtonians riding out to see the spectacle of it all. The battle and the long war that followed turned out to be more tragic than anyone expected.

Of course, this is a work of fiction and some events have been tweaked here and there to fit the story. For those who want to learn more about the actual battle, you can find several interesting accounts of wartime Washington and the events surrounding Bull Run. Time and again, I find myself referring to *Reveille in Washington* by Margaret Leech for a civilian perspective of the war and its personalities.

Finally, I wanted to express gratitude to the advance readers who were so helpful with the timeline and other details. Flynn and I can't thank you enough!

—D.H.

ABOUT THE AUTHOR

David Healey lives in Maryland, where he worked as a journalist for more than twenty years. He is a member of the International Thriller Writers and a contributing editor to *The Big Thrill* magazine. Join his newsletter list at:

www.davidhealeyauthor.com
or
www.facebook.com/david.healey.books

Made in United States
North Haven, CT
08 January 2024

47170948R00124